SHANNON'S LUCK

To: Marie -
Thank you for
your support &
Happy Reading

Debbie Isbell
2017
xx

DEBBIE ISBELL

SHANNON'S LUCK

© Copyright 2016 Debbie Isbell

ISBN-13: 978-1533224538 (CreateSpace-Assigned)

ISBN-10: 1533224536

Formatted by Ready, Set, Edit

For David—one of the luckiest days of my life was the day you walked in.

CHAPTER ONE

It was just past dawn on what was already starting out to be a very hot, sticky day. The weather report called for unseasonably hot temperatures for a March morning in Abilene, Texas. Janelle Beckett got up earlier than usual because she did not want to miss one minute of her two month vacation. The vacation was a reward from a partner at the law firm, Raskins & Caine, P.C., where Janelle had been employed for about three years.

For over eighteen months the law firm—sometimes Janelle felt like that meant her alone—had been involved in a large oil battle between an apparent sheik who had never been to Texas and a local rancher who was not willing to back down. Everything is bigger in Texas they say; this lawsuit was no exception. Janelle had been forced into countless hours of research, briefs, memoranda and rewrites, along with hours of discussion between the young ambitious lawyer, Scott Raskins, who was making quite a name for himself battling the oil community, and herself.

Janelle laughed at these thoughts and mumbled, "Well,

the hours aren't totally countless, I had to bill for every one of them!" Janelle stared at her reflection in the mirror. She pulled her shoulder length light brown hair into a pony tail. The dark blue eyes staring back at her were tired and lacked the sparkle they had always held in the past. The dark circles under her eyes had become more pronounced with each passing month. Janelle thought she looked at least ten years older than she really was.

Going on about her business, Janelle went humming quietly to herself. Janelle had been running on coffee and fast food for months. The diet she had maintained, mixed with her severe lack of any quality sleep, and the reading of every case filed in the courts of Texas to even mentioned the word "oil," had landed Janelle the coveted promotion she would be coming back to after her vacation: Lead Litigation Assistant to Scott Raskins. Her hard work and dedication had been rewarded with a very large raise, a new office on the exclusive 17th Floor and the two month vacation to the location of her choice.

Finally, the case and trial were over and another rancher in Texas became rich off the ever flowing "black gold" of the Texas hills. "Well," she said out loud to no one in particular, "you deserve the peace and quiet girl, get to it!!"

No one could believe Janelle did not choose to travel to Italy, or Spain, or France, or the Bahamas, or even Hawaii for that matter. Janelle wanted peace and quiet; no phones and a lot of nature. All of those coveted and popular vacation spots had too many people and too many events or sights a tourist could not miss out on while there. She knew herself well. If Janelle went somewhere within an arm's length of tourist attractions and museums, she would be on the go from sunrise to sunset—checking every location off her list. No, a packed schedule isn't what was called for this time. Escape - that is what she wanted. Escape from deadlines, telephones, lawyers, oil, ranchers, secretaries, paralegals, investigators, computers and paper! And escape Janelle would.

As Janelle got in the brand new black and shiny BMW—another component of her bonus from Scott Raskins—and headed out of her neighborhood she remembered the countless discussions about her travel plans that had turned into arguments with her older sister. Janelle had a moment of guilt about the breaking point she reached with her sister, Sarah, just last night. Sarah was older than Janelle by two years, but she was certainly the more carefree sister.

***

"Janelle, you have two months off, all expenses paid before you have to be at school, and you are going to hibernate in the mountains of Arizona," Sarah exclaimed loudly with all the exuberance that usually made Janelle love her even more, but not this time. "Janelle, I would fly to every place I ever wanted to go over the course of the first six weeks and then go back and spend the last two weeks at the place I enjoyed the most. Janelle, go to Athens, France, Rome, Sweden, leave the United States, Janelle, anywhere but a cabin in Arizona. No one would pick a cabin in the woods over the vacation of a lifetime!" By now Sarah was pacing and animating her conversation with her arms flying about her as she punctuated her speech with hand gestures. Sarah's waist length auburn hair tossed around her body as she paced and lectured her sister. Her voice had escalated in her attempt to convince Janelle to take the trip of a life time.

Janelle always envied her more beautiful, taller sister.

3

This was not the thought going through her mind as she felt trapped by the conversation she was having...correction, the lecture she was getting from Sarah.

"Sarah," Janelle exclaimed much louder and sounding much harsher than she intended. She lowered her voice to a whisper, closed her eyes, put her hands out as if to motion "stop." "Enough, ok? I am going to Arizona. I'm going to the mountains. I need a break. I need to just rest and not have to think. Not to have to go. Not to have to do. Not to have to report. Don't you realize I have spent well over a year and a half with my nose in law books reading every case filed since Adam and Eve who, mind you, did not discover oil in the Garden of Eden? I have met countless deadlines, attended meetings, depositions, and court hearings. I have been yelled at by so many people for so many reasons I now jump every time I hear my name, Scott's name, our client's name, or even the word "oil." I have dreaded every time Scott walked up to me yelling my name, dreaded every phone call put through to me, invented strategies where none existed, and turned sows ears into silk purses. I have begged ranchers to believe that Scott was doing what was best, begged them to do things they did not want to do and tried to convince them they would not regret it. I have been screamed at by those same people when it appeared the promises I made were not coming to fruition. I have interviewed and questioned so many people I don't even know how many, and I don't know how many barely even spoke English. I have eaten whatever they put in front of me, whenever it was put in front of me. I have worked well into the night only to find people coming back to work in the morning and I had not yet gone home. Or people would come to the office in the morning and find me asleep at my desk drooling on my hand. Well, if you could call a thirty minute nap after an eighteen hour day sleeping. Of course this was before Scott, who was also carrying the burden of responsibility, would lose it over something that he didn't like or we had no control over, or when he decided he wanted the two hundredth rewrite of a two hundred page long document, and then rewrite, rewrite, rewrite!" Janelle was the one pacing and yelling now, not at Sarah, but to her. "You may recall, sister dear, when this case started I was in my first semester of law school when one of the partners told me my schooling was interfering with my ability to commit to this case. I had a choice, my job or my schooling. My life and schooling went on hold. Not to mention the fact about ten months ago Glenn decided he couldn't tolerate my work schedule and the fact we never saw each other. Remember he decided he wanted to see other people. I haven't even had a chance to cry over that one yet, Sarah. Don't you see? I. Have. Had it! Dropping out of sight is the only way I can reclaim my life and it sounds great to me. Going barefoot, wearing jeans, smelling pine trees and listening to peace and quiet in a little A Frame cabin that faces a stream sounds like a dream come true to me. Watching animals in the woods and the peace of a sunrise or sunset from my porch is all I want to commit to right now. Once I have a chance to unwind and get back in touch with myself I will be ready to start law school - again." Janelle's voice had lowered and tears were running down her flushed cheeks. Janelle took a deep breath and slowly, dramatically exhaled before continuing. She turned and walked toward her sister. "I'm sorry, Sarah, but I have nothing left. I am twenty-three years old, Sarah, and I feel I am going on fifty right now. I just have nothing left."

Sarah realized she had pushed her sister too far. She

didn't mean to hurt her. She wanted a hectic, fun-filled, go every minute, event filled vacation for Janelle. The 'vacation of a life time' she kept calling it. For Janelle, right now, this just wasn't to be. "Go to Flagstaff, baby sister. Rest. I love you." The sisters hugged and Janelle cherished the feeling of her sister's love coming through the embrace. The girls looked at each other and laughed.

"Finally, you understand!" Janelle giggled and her nose wrinkled as she laughed. "I love you too, but I'm leaving in the morning. Are you going to help me pack or not?"

"Sure, which suitcase?" Sarah was relieved the tense moment had passed and the wrinkled nose smile told her Janelle wasn't angry.

"Suitcase nothing, I want four pairs of jeans, two pairs or shorts, a week's worth of underclothes and socks, my tennis shoes, sandals, and hiking boots, roll them all up and stuff them in the duffle bag already on my bed. I have already packed shirts and a jacket. I will finish with the bathroom stuff. You will of course notice I am not taking anything that resembles a dress, a suit, high heels, nylons or make up! Clean, pure and simple. That is what this next two months is about," Janelle said genuinely smiling. "When my vacation is over I'll come back and get organized to set up my new apartment and new life as a law student in Tempe, Arizona."

"So Janelle, are you going to actually drive that shiny new car to Arizona or are you going to get dropped from an airplane somewhere in the vicinity of where you actually intend to stay?" Sarah's singsong voice teased and Janelle knew it. Yes, everything was okay between the sisters.

"Well, packing is finished and I'm starving, Janelle. Can I talk you in to dinner and a movie before you leave me?

6

Consider it a farewell gesture. I don't really know what I'm going to do not seeing or talking to you every day." Sarah batted her eyes to keep the tears, threatening to fall, from doing so.

"Sarah, you haven't hardly gotten more than two or three minutes of my time for ages. I plan on saving my last week of vacation to come back and do nothing but hang out with you! Besides you'll be fine! If you happen to get lost while you are out driving and find yourself around the Arizona vicinity, come see me." Dinner and a movie would have to wait.

CHAPTER TWO

After hours of driving, stopping, reading maps and rereading maps, Janelle finally saw the sign that said "Entering Flagstaff Population..." Well, that would remain a mystery for the time being. Everyone drives too fast past signs to read them.

Well, Janelle thought to herself, *whatever the population of Flagstaff was when I zoomed past that sign, it is one more for now.*

Janelle decided to stop at a small restaurant bar she saw along the road. "Shannon's Luck," she read out loud. Sounded like the perfect place for her to stop and have an early dinner. Janelle decided this would be the perfect place to regroup and review her map. She pulled her once shiny, now very dusty, BMW into the parking lot and slowly stepped out. Reaching for the sky and rotating her stiff neck in circles, Janelle could feel the driving fatigue leaving her body already. This would be a perfect place to stop before finishing the drive to her home away from home.

"Shannon's Luck" looked like a quaint old place. It

looked as if it had been built from old barn wood, or perhaps it had stood for so long the original wood had faded to the amazing gray-brown color it was now. The metal had a green-gray patina which only comes from age. This place had charm and as Janelle approached she saw it was actually two stories, not just the one you first see from the road. It was much bigger than she originally thought. Not sure which level she was allowed to enter she headed to the top floor street level. Janelle stopped and smiled at two dogs tied up outside the front door. They were the epitome of cattle dogs. Both had long fur with a mixture of browns and greys and whites and blacks. When the larger dog looked up at her she realized it had two different colored eyes. For some reason the dog made Janelle smile.

As Janelle entered the restaurant she saw the old wooden bar across from the door; a bar that probably seated only ten-to-fifteen people. There were eight tables, each set for four, each with a red checkered tablecloth, silverware settings and flowers tucked in clear glass vases.   Menus were tucked between the napkin holder and the condiment holder.

The bartender called to her with an inviting smile in his voice, "Welcome to Shannon's Luck. What can I interest you in little miss?"

Janelle smiled and walked closer to the bar. She smiled at the balding older man as she leaned against a bar stool. "Hi, I am passing through and wanted a cold drink and a light meal."

"Well, I am Frank, and you are in the right place. Have a seat and let me buy you something cold to drink. Beer, wine?"

"No," Janelle said smiling. Janelle knew she had more

driving to do and was tired from being behind the wheel of the car for so many hours and days. A perfect glass of wine would send her to sleep. "I better save the liquid refreshment for when I reach my destination. Could I just have an iced tea or a diet drink?"

Frank replied, "You are welcome to whatever quenches your thirst. I will get your drink while you look over the menu. There is one to your left next to the napkin holder."

When Janelle turned to reach for the menu she observed a rough, leathered skinned old man, with a long unkempt beard. He reminded her of an old rusty pirate. He had kind eyes that boasted of a long, hard life well lived. Well, it could have been his exaggerated hand movements or loud voice that boasted of the life well lived.

Janelle watched the old man flirting with a young woman who must have been a waitress there. The young waitress flirted back as if this old man were a handsome young stud she wanted to be courted by. The genuineness of the obvious friendship the two shared made Janelle smile. She wanted simple laughter. Joking and nothing too serious to talk about, just being able to enjoy another person's easy company. There was a sincerity between them which you could feel in the air as they interacted. These people were simply loved for being who they were on the inside. There was no pretense or shallowness with these people. Janelle suddenly felt very alone.

"Decide what you want to have?" Frank's word's interrupted her roaming thoughts.

"Oh, sorry, I was wandering and haven't even looked at the menu. I am pretty sure I would like a burger and a side salad of some kind," she replied hoping her sad moment didn't come across in her voice. Janelle wasn't one for feeling sorry for herself and she certainly didn't intend to start now.

"One hamburger on its way." The bartender disappeared to turn in her order. The look on her face before he interrupted her thoughts hit him hard. A woman should never look as tired and alone as she did at that moment. He wondered what her story was, but knew he would probably never know. Most people who just passed through never were to be seen again.

Janelle had enjoyed a glass of cold tea and just received her refill when her food arrived. "What is downstairs?" She asked Frank as he sat the plate in front of her.

"More formal dining," Frank replied. "We serve Italian food downstairs. You could order the same things up here if you wanted. We found that not everyone can climb down the wooden staircase, so we turned the upstairs bar into a bar and restaurant. Would you rather move down there, or are you ok eating up here with me for company?" Frank chuckled.

"Oh I am fine, I just wondered if I came in the correct door." She smiled, and he saw that she looked stressed as well as tired and alone.

"Enjoy your meal little Missy. I will be back after I get that other couple their food and you can tell me the story about why you are passing through my bar." Frank smiled, winked, and walked away.

While Janelle sat enjoying her burger a man sitting at a table behind her spoke. His voice sounded like he seduced people with the deep growl of his voice for a living. She heard him ask a question, "So, are you trying to find out how to stay around town, or how to get the hell out?"

Janelle turned in her seat and was caught by the smile in his deep sensual voice and for some reason she chose to answer him. "I am trying to make sure I take the right road only a little way out of town. I am new around here and don't want to get lost my first day here." She smiled back at him.

The redness of her eyes, and the dark circles under Janelle's eyes, made her look tired. The tightness of her jaw, even as she smiled, made her look stressed. As he looked at her, Logan thought she looked way too responsible. She was beautiful. She needed a man to help her find her way. Logan shook his head to quickly dislodge that thought before it got him in trouble.

"So," he drawled with what he hoped sounded only a little like he was flirting, "I have been around here my whole life. I know pretty much everywhere you could possibly be going. Want some confirmation on your travel plans?"

Why did she trust him instantly? She wasn't reckless by nature. Something about the small town atmosphere to make a girl feel safe and trusting of tall, dark, and bearded strangers.

"Well, I have rented a small A Frame cabin for two months. The directions refer a lot to turning on forest roads and looking for certain mile posts. I wanted to be sure I knew where I was going before I took off further down the road." The information poured out of her as if he was an old friend and not a friendly stranger.

"Whose cabin?" His voice sounded like he was offering a flirting challenge.

She parried. "His name is Carlos Mendoza."

"Carlos and Lepita Mendoza? Well I have known Carlos my entire life. Whole lot of good people those two. I can tell you exactly how to get there." And he did.

Sarah thanked Frank for the food and iced tea, which

he insisted on not charging her for if she would promise to come back and buy a drink when she was more familiar with her surroundings. She stood and turned toward Logan. She started to thank the handsome man who had helped her with directions to the cabin, but realized there had been no offering of a name between them.

"I want to thank you for all of your help in reviewing the map with me, and pointing out the grocery store. My name is Janelle, by the way. I didn't catch your name, so I can't properly thank you." She smiled as she spoke.

He looked at her and his dark eyes sparkled. She knew he was thinking something playful, but she didn't want to be a tease. She wanted to get her necessary items and get to the cabin so she could take a long, hot, relaxing bath. "I don't have to have a name, I guess. So, thank you." She tilted her head as she talked, nodded once, and then turned quickly to walk toward the door.

"My name is Logan. I was thinking that if you wanted to thank me properly you would let me buy you dinner and a drink sometime while you are in town," he called out as she walked away.

Janelle stopped before reaching for the door handle. She pivoted on one leg to turn back to look at that amazingly handsome man. "I don't know that I will actually get back to town much. My plan is to pretty much stay in the woods," she replied. He looked almost hurt. "If I do get to town, and if you're around, I will let you buy me dinner, but only to thank you properly." She tilted her head slightly and smiled a small smile as she spoke. Her nose wrinkled, as it always did, when her smile was sincere.

My God, she mumbled in her own mind, *I'm flirting.* What was it about this man that made Janelle feel she had known him forever? He stood staring at her with a half-smile on his handsome face and she felt like an idiot.

"Well, Logan, thank you again. I best be going. I don't really want to drive somewhere unfamiliar in the dark. It was nice to meet you both." She smiled at the leathered old man as she turned to leave. He smiled a toothless grin. Janelle wished she knew his story.

Janelle drove away from the restaurant relaxed and happy. She easily found the little grocery store both Logan and Frank had told her she would pass while driving. She picked up a week's worth of necessary food and supplies. She probably should get more, but decided it would be nice to come to town once or twice. Given how friendly Frank had been to her, even knowing she was from out of state, Janelle knew she would want to come back and see him again. She didn't want to acknowledge the voice in her head telling her she wouldn't mind seeing that handsome Logan again either.

Janelle's mind was hooked on thinking about Logan and it wasn't budging. He certainly was a man to remember. Was it legal for a man to have deep hazel eyes the color of his? He had to be 6'4" tall. Through his faded and tight-fitting jeans, Logan looked as if he had powerful thighs that came from long days of honest hard work. She had never really known anyone that wore facial hair. His dark brown mustache and close cut beard added to his charm. Did he look a little dangerous? She wasn't sure. Did he seem brotherly? That wasn't it. *Stop it!* Janelle finally reigned in her roaming thoughts about Logan. *You are here to rest, not get all tied up in knots over a gorgeous cowboy in jeans and a beard, Janelle,* she scolded herself out loud.

So, with her appetite satisfied and her car packed with

the groceries she had purchased, confident in her ability to find the cabin with what remained of the daylight, Janelle set off for the final couple miles of driving to find her temporary home for the next two months.

CHAPTER THREE

Janelle never saw the eighteen wheel truck as it rounded the winding road and lost control, careening straight into the vehicle in front of her. It all happened too fast for anyone to react, although Janelle did have time for one thought to register—don't drive off the edge of the road.

A total of four cars fell victim to the horrific accident. Janelle's BMW was trapped between the small pick-up that took the worst of the accident and the van that violently hit her from behind. There was no hope for whoever was in that small truck. Janelle was losing consciousness and had no idea of anyone's fate, including her own. Her last conscious thought was about the horror her family would suffer knowing she had died.

The accident had blocked all lanes of traffic and several cars were forced to stop. A few Good Samaritans rushed over to the injured passengers to see if they could do anything to help. Out of a small dark blue Dodge Dakota pickup came a man instinctively ran to Janelle's car. He pushed his way past the onlookers and the people who were actually trying to help. He shouted "don't move anyone." He was almost to Janelle's car when he yelled to the man leaning through the window of her car. "Don't touch her. I know her, let me through."

What Logan saw certainly caught him off guard. He was used to the controlled atmosphere of his ranch and running his office. He had seen some pretty messed up people in bar fights, but nothing prepared him to see the angle at which Janelle's neck was tilted. He was sure it was broken. He was sure she was dead. As he looked at Janelle he saw the steering wheel lodged tightly against her chest. He instinctively reached for her neck to check for a pulse. Janelle had a large, deep gash on the right top of her head. Blood was pouring from the gash and she was losing a lot of blood. Logan saw the white color of bone and realized it was a horribly deep wound. The deformed angle of her legs stuck beneath the car's dash was evidence of two broken legs. Her right shoulder and arm hung at a strange angle and looked dislocated from its socket. Just as the thought crossed Logan's mind that Janelle not surviving her injuries may be for the best, he felt the tiny jump of blood under his finger still lingering on her throat. Blood was actually jumping through her tiny, blood stained, neck. His own heart almost stopped as he realized Janelle was alive. He took a deep breath not realizing he had been holding it in. He quickly pulled off his flannel shirt and tied it around Janelle's head trying to stop some of the bleeding. As his thoughts rushed about what to do next an emergency response crew was standing behind him and talking to him. Logan had no idea what they were saying. He just stood staring at Janelle and then slowly backed away as the emergency responders moved in to take over.

"You need to help this lady right now, she may not

make it otherwise." Logan heard one paramedic say to another.

"We will handle it from here, Logan. You need to step away," another paramedic said as he put his hand on Logan's shoulder. Logan didn't move. The paramedic spoke to Logan again. Logan looked more like a scared teenager standing there watching the car while the paramedics worked on Janelle instead of the always in control man they knew him to be. "Logan, you are going to have to back away to let them work."

Other paramedics disbursed the crowd as two of them checked and confirmed the man in the eighteen wheeler had not survived and neither had the man in the small truck in front of Janelle.

Logan did step back, but stayed close enough to hear Captain Meyer whisper to his fellow paramedic with an exhaled defeated breath, "We may lose her when we remove the steering wheel. Is he family?"

"No," Logan answered from where he was standing. "I just met her, I was making sure she got to the Mendoza rental cabin. She is a visitor in town and didn't know her way. I can't believe she is still alive. I need to stay with her. She doesn't know anyone here in Flagstaff."

"Will to live, it saves the weak from the strong," Captain Meyer said as he and another paramedic began to cut away the steering wheel.

Miraculously the steering wheel was not imbedded, but was tightly pushed against Janelle's chest. She was free of the steering wheel and she was alive. The paramedics placed a cervical collar around her neck before starting to carefully remove her from the car. Once free, they placed her on a back board. They knew something was terribly wrong with her neck. The angle and the way it moved when they put the cervical collar around her neck spoke to the senior paramedic of all the broken neck injuries he had seen. He knew something was different because she was alive. Her vital signs were surprisingly good for the injuries Janelle had sustained. The senior paramedic realized Janelle's head almost looked as if it were decapitated even though it remained attached to her body. These patients never survived. It always ended the same. After she was secured on the board, the paramedics began to treat the worst of her wounds to stop the bleeding and stabilize broken bones. They started an IV and placed her on monitors to watch and make sure she continued breathing and her heart kept beating. She had an oxygen mask on her face. They all silently prayed they could save her.

As they moved her to the air ambulance, Captain Meyer called ahead to the Flagstaff Medical Center Emergency Room. Logan stood watching and it seemed everything was occurring in slow motion. His senses were heightened and he honed in quickly when he heard Captain Meyer begin speaking. What Logan heard made him feel as if an anvil was being dropped on his chest.

"Female, early 20's, severe injuries, head wound, broken ribs, leg, arm, and probable internal decapitation."

An Air Evac helicopter arrived and Captain Meyer called to his paramedics wheeling Janelle toward the ambulance. "Take her in the helicopter. She won't survive the drive." The paramedics turned and quickly wheeled Janelle to the Air Evac helicopter. The blades of the helicopter were still turning and the strong movement of air shook Logan back to the present and out of his fog.

Another paramedic walked up and told Captain Meyer

there were two survivors from the van behind Janelle, two children, neither of the parents survived. The severity of some of these accidents never ceased to tug at the hearts of the paramedics, but those emotions were tucked away until their job was completed and the injured were treated and released from their care. Remembering the trauma and the horror of these tragedies was usually done by each of the first responders later in solitude.

The orphaned children would certainly come back to mind and this poor woman who probably would not survive the night, or if she did, will never be the same.

The children were also transported to the hospital for treatment of their injuries. Sheriff's deputies were everywhere. Logan heard a sheriff's deputy mention they believed the driver of the eighteen wheeler had fallen asleep behind the wheel. Witnesses had seen him weaving a mile or so back as he drove.

Logan somehow felt responsible to notify Janelle's family. He walked back over to her vehicle and looked in the front seat for her purse or anything that would tell him how to reach her family. He found her purse and a small duffle bag. He grabbed them both and started back to his vehicle. He knew that she would be taken into surgery immediately, if she survived the trip in the Air Evac. He decided to go to the hospital to see if he could help her or find out who her family was so that someone could be notified. The plates on her car were from Texas he realized as the tow trucks separated the cars. That was a start. It seemed that the only thing that mattered to him now was that Janelle survive.

When Logan reached the hospital he went straight to the E.R. and asked about Janelle, fortunately the nurse he approached knew him and since he was asking, she just accepted that he was family.

"Logan, there is a problem. The doctor will be out to talk to you soon," the nurse reported.

Logan sat in the waiting room. Dr. Patrick walked out and asked for him by name. "She is still in surgery. She had not regained any form of consciousness. There was a lot of damage to her skull. Our biggest problem is that she has an internal decapitation. That is the neck is separated, the muscles are all torn from bone and the only thing keeping it all together is the skin around her neck. I am not going to lie to you Logan, most people do not survive this. One wrong move and the nervous system ceases and she no longer breathes and her heart will no longer beat. The surgical team is placing six screw in her skull in a type of halo brace until further decisions can be made. The x-ray series revealed her head is completely severed from her spine. Fortunately her spinal cord and nerves are completely intact. She appears to respond to touch and sensation. How are you related to her? Do you know how to reach her closest family?" The doctor's words echoed in Logan's ear as if they were coming out of another room.

"No, Dr. Patrick, no. I feel like I will though. There is nothing to make a man feel more useless than these moments right here. I just met her at Dad's place and was following her out to the Mendoza's cabin when this accident happened. I brought her duffle bag and purse from the car. The sheriff had his hands full and I figured they would show up here to see if she survives. Maybe you, or the sheriff can find the information you need in this bag." Logan talked with no emotion. Why did he feel so numbed by this event? "I am not usually a helpless man, Doc, and I can't do anything but stand by and wait until someone tells me her fate." Logan turned over the duffle bag and purse and said he would hang around until someone knew more.

"Sounds to me, Logan, if you don't mind my saying so, that the good Lord put this lady in your way and in your heart. Maybe you are to learn something from this. I will tell you one thing she is a fighter. Used to be that only one or two patients ever left the accident scene alive with these injuries. Now we do see them and I have heard that there are new procedures to help repair this damage. I don't want to give you false hope. Usually the prognosis is very bleak." Dr. Patrick tried to smile a reassuring smile as he reached over and touched Logan's shoulder.

"I will wait," Logan whispered standing with his hat in his hand, turning it around and around by the brim, for his own comfort as the doctor spoke. Logan finally went to sit in the patient waiting area.

Several hours passed and Janelle was very weak, but the gash on her head was sutured, her broken bones were all repaired, all major bleeding had been stopped and she was alive. After surgery Janelle was moved to the ICU and amazingly she was breathing on her own. The only problem that remained was the internal decapitation. This would be the deciding factor in whether or not Janelle survived. Dr. Patrick knew from a Medical Review Journal article he had recently read that there was a young doctor at St. Joseph's Hospital in Phoenix who had performed the operation to repair an internal decapitation a handful of times. He had lost two patients and one was permanently disabled, but the article did speak of two successful surgeries with successful outcomes that restored his patients to health. This doctor had utilized a new procedure to reattach the skull to the spine. Instead of the usual hooks, plates and horseshoe shaped rods used in prior attempted surgeries, the doctor had used two titanium screws to hold a young teenaged man's skull in place.

The EEG indicated that Janelle had good brain activity, but she was being kept in an induced coma.

"Dr. Patrick," the nurse spoke quietly, knowing she was interrupting his thoughts, "The Sheriff is waiting to see you. He wants to know what to tell her family." Dr. Patrick walked toward the doctor's lounge without offering a response to the nurse.

As Dr. Patrick approached, the sheriff stood and reached out his hand. "Geoff," he said, "Tell me it was you who operated and that she survived, I have to call her family and don't want to tell them otherwise."

"She is alive. Weak, in an induced coma and about to face a very important night. She IS alive though. We have a terrible problem. She has an internal decapitation. I am going to call Dr. Curtis at St. Joe's in Phoenix for an emergency consultation and then I will call her family. I want to have something to tell them. Give them not only the horrific news, but some hope." Dr. Patrick closed his eyes and rubbed his temples. "I hate car accidents."

"Thank God," the Sheriff exclaimed, "by the way it is sure great to see you Geoff. That was an awful accident. And I hate them too. As they go, this was a bad one. There were four vehicles involved, everyone dead except the two kids that are in your E.R. now and this little lady. I am so relieved she is still alive."

"Well, let me make the calls." Dr. Patrick turned and walked away. He thought of being young and getting in trouble as a teenage boy with the sheriff. That seemed a life time ago.

Dr. Patrick dialed the phone to St. Joe's—Barrows Hospital in Phoenix. It happened that Dr. Curtis was on duty when he called, but was in with patients. Dr. Patrick left a message to call as soon as possible regarding an emergency consultation. He sat in his office working on patient charts and waited for the call.

CHAPTER FOUR

As Dr. Patrick hung up from his hour long conversation with Dr. Curtis he felt the first ray of hope for Janelle. She seemed strong and healthy. Dr. Curtis would have her transported to St. Joseph's by Air Evac first thing Monday morning. After evaluation and determining if Janelle was a good candidate for the surgery, he would call and arrange a meeting with the family. This surgery was still in early stages, but provided her the only hope for life over death she was going to get. With the information from Dr. Curtis, Dr. Patrick felt a little more positive about his call to the family. It was time to make that call.

The Sheriff and Logan had provided Dr. Patrick with the information they knew and from information in Janelle's wallet. Her cellphone was crushed and unfortunately of no use. There was a business card in her wallet that listed her name: "Janelle L. Beckett." It listed her employer and with no "in case of emergency" names or phone numbers in her wallet and an unusable phone, Dr. Patrick had no choice but to call her employer, Scott Raskins. It was Saturday evening and he doubted he would reach anyone. The best he could do was leave a message and see if he could locate any additional information on her family. He would try to find Scott Raskins' home number through information.

When voicemail answered, Dr. Patrick left a cautious message, "Scott Raskins. This is Dr. Geoff Patrick. I am a surgeon at the Flagstaff Medical Center. It is extremely urgent that I speak with you regarding Janelle Beckett. There has been an accident and I must contact her family. Please call the hospital and have me paged immediately." Dr. Patrick left the phone number of the hospital and went to check on the children who were involved in the accident. He was told the children's aunt and uncle lived in Flagstaff and were now at the hospital.

CHAPTER FIVE

Sarah Beckett was singing to herself in her third floor apartment as she picked up the weeks clothes from the floor, newspapers and mail. It was 5:00 a.m. and it was Sunday finally. She held an old blanket close and drifted back to the day he asked her out.

"Hi, Sarah, can I talk to you for a minute?" Mitch Hansen asked. Every day for two months he had made it a point to smile at everyone in the office when he walked by and Sarah had made it a point to always at least say "hi" in return in hopes Mitch would notice her. Now he wanted to talk to her.

"Sure," Sarah whispered, almost forgetting to breathe.

He smiled at her and she thought he looked like a shy school boy instead of a business man in his thirties. *He HAS to ask me out,* she screamed in her own mind.

"I was wondering, Sarah," he paused. And then continued "Do you like horses much?" His eyebrow raised as he asked the question which she thought made him look even more handsome.

***

Sarah had to hold herself back from throwing herself in his arms and kissing him. "I love horses—love riding horses."

"Great," he smiled and his confidence appeared to return. I was wondering if you would like to go on a breakfast ride with me Sunday morning. I know you sister is leaving Saturday so I thought Sunday would be better. I know it is short notice, I would normally not wait until Thursday to ask you, but I just...."

"I would love to!" Sarah didn't even let him finish the question. *Great.*

"Great," he smiled and continued "I will have to pick you up at 6:00 a.m. I will call you here tomorrow for your address and directions to your house, okay?"

He had been true to his word and called her Friday morning before 10:00. Now it was Sunday and less than forty-five minutes until he arrived and this dream she had replayed for months would begin to unfold. Sarah walked to her hall closet mirror and looked herself over carefully.

She nodded approvingly. Sarah had taken special care to pick out the right outfit and had pulled her long auburn hair into a loose braid. *Yes*, she thought to herself, *you did well in picking this outfit. I hope you agree Mitch*, she stated out loud to no one there except her silly Siamese cat, Moe.

It was then that the doorbell rang. Sarah glanced at the old wall clock and saw it was 5:50 a.m. "Thank you for being early," she said quietly in the direction of the front door.

As Sarah opened the front door her knees went weak. "You look incredible Mitch," she exclaimed with what she knew was too much honest exuberance. "I am so used to seeing you in business suits. Please, come in."

28

"Ditto and damn! I knew I should have stuck with the grey pin stripes." They both laughed with an unusual comfort neither of them felt when he asked her out or when she accepted. The two didn't know each other very well, but that was something they both wanted to change.

Mitch thought to himself as he looked at Sarah with her "yes I have been awake for a while, but it is still very early morning" sleepy smile, that he was so very happy he finally asked her out.

"This is going to be such a perfect day, Mitch," Sarah said excitedly. "I have been looking forward to going out with you for so long." As soon as the last three words were out of her mouth she groaned inside. "Sorry," she said. "I guess I should have kept that to myself." She laughed embarrassed. Sometimes she thought she acted more like fifteen than twenty-five.

"Never apologize for honesty, Sarah. Especially when I get a compliment out of it," Mitch said sincerely and winked at her. He stood, hands on his hips and holding an intense gaze. He didn't smile, didn't laugh. He just stood there and soaked up the moment. Mitch knew he owed her something verbal to make the moment less tense and embarrassing for her, but he could think of nothing to say that wouldn't make the moment more uncomfortable, so instead he chose a teasing reply that he immediately regretted because it didn't sound as playful as he intended. "I guess I should have gotten here earlier."

Sarah looked down embarrassed. Mitch took two steps and closed the gap between himself and Sarah. He touched her shoulder. That was the gesture she needed.

***

Sarah and Mitch shared their life stories as they rode

horses along the countryside. They talked about each other, their life, dreams, fears, goals, hobbies, work, friends and family. Sarah told him all about her parents and her little sister, Janelle. Mitch had heard Sarah telling a co-worker her sister was leaving town on Saturday. Sarah filled him in on the remaining details of where Janelle had gone and why she chose a remote getaway.

Mitch told Sarah he was the middle child of five children. Mitch had twin brothers two years older than he, David and Daniel, and a younger sister, Hope and a younger brother, James. James, he told Sarah, was only seven and quite a surprise to the family. Everyone adored him. Mitch obviously loved his family and they both enjoyed life in general. They were a good match. Finally, they decided, without speaking, to stop and stretch their legs.

It seemed to be a natural progression of their day together when Mitch took Sarah's hand as they walked beside the horses. Neither of them felt the need to talk anymore as they walked. Anyone walking by would have thought them to have been growing in their love for years.

After they had walked beside the horses for about thirty minutes Mitch turned and walked in front of her and stopped, facing her. Janelle stopped short and giggled thinking Mitch was playing. He smiled slightly, and then gently, so very gently, lifted her chin toward his mouth, dipped his head and kissed her. As suddenly as Mitch started the kiss, he ended it. Mitch turned, still holding her hand, and started slowly walking again. Sarah felt warm everywhere and felt very foolish when she felt a tear slide down her cheek. This was the happiest she had been in a very long time.

CHAPTER SIX

Scott Raskins went to his office every day. Weekends and holidays meant nothing to him. The only difference this Sunday was Janelle would not be there with him. It has been a very long time since Scott was alone in his office. He knew she certainly earned her BMW bonus and he was only too happy to pay for her vacation. She was going to make a brilliant lawyer and he hoped she would return to Raskins and Caine after completing law school and becoming licensed.

Scott decided to check messages, return a few phone calls and read his mail, then he was going to get out of the office for a long restful afternoon of golf. He had not played in over a year. His game was certainly going to show it. Scott retrieved several normal messages from the same clients that call every weekend shocked that no one was answering. Then he heard Dr. Patrick's message. He immediately wrote down the number and dialed the hospital in Flagstaff.

The hospital operator quickly patched Scott through to Dr. Patrick's office.

"Dr. Patrick," he announced.

"Hello, Dr. Patrick, this is Scott Raskins. I am returning your call regarding Jani Beckett, er, I'm sorry, Janelle Beckett. Is she ok? What happened?" His normal calm legal demeanor was nowhere to be found as he rifled off anxious questions.

"Thank you for calling back, Mr. Raskins." Dr. Patrick knew from years of giving bad news that the slower and more calmly he spoke the more he would control the situation. "Janelle was in a very serious automobile accident. It is actually a miracle she is alive right now. I am trying to reach a family member. Do you know who I can contact?"

Scott was trying to process the words "miracle she is alive." He was silent. He didn't respond. Actually, his ears had started buzzing so loudly after those words he heard nothing else.

"Mr. Raskins? Do you know who might be her next of kin?" Dr. Patrick asked hoping to snap Scott back from the news he had just been given.

"Oh my God, oh my God," Scott stammered. "Yes, yes, she has family. I'm sorry. She has parents and a sister. Her parents are elderly and I would be uncomfortable calling them first with this news. I don't know how they will react. Her sister will be the best first contact. Although she is going to just die when she hears this. I should be there or at least on the line when you call her. Would you mind if I call her and conference her in?" Scott asked.

"Certainly," Dr. Patrick was able to impart patience and empathy speaking just one word.

Scott called Sarah's number to add her to the call with Dr. Patrick. There was no answer. Scott left a message asking Sarah to call him on his cellphone as soon as she received the message. He didn't want to leave a message in any detail to scare her, but he did need her to understand the urgency.

"Hi Sarah, this is Scott Raskins," he began, hesitating, waiting for the exact right words to come to mind, "will you please call me as soon as possible. It is urgent that I speak with you. Please call me on my cellphone whatever time you get this. Please."

Scott disconnected Sarah from the call and again he was on the phone with Dr. Patrick. "There was no answer. I don't have her cell phone number. I left a message asking her to call. I told her it was urgent."

"Do you have her parents' phone number? I think it is important to reach someone as soon as possible."

"I will drive to Sarah's house. If she still isn't home I will drive to her parents and tell them in person. It will take about twenty minutes to get to Sarah's house."

"Thank you Mr. Raskins, please have either Sarah or her parents call me and have me paged if I am not in my office."

Scott hesitated in saying good-bye. He knew he should let the doctor off the call, but he had to ask. "Dr. Patrick?" He just couldn't say the words.

After too long a pause, Dr. Patrick filled the gap. "Did you have a question, Mr. Raskins?"

Scott slowly drew as much air into his lungs as was possible for them to hold and spoke reverently, "Is she going to die?" Although speaking quietly, the shaking fear in his voice came through loudly.

"I'm sorry, Mr. Raskins, I can't answer that question. Thank you for contacting her sister. I will await a call from her family. Again, be sure they ask to have me paged."

The response did nothing to settle the horrific fear festering in Scott's belly. "I will. Thank you." Scott wasn't sure if he actually said the words out loud, or just thought them. All he knew was the line had disconnected and he had to reach Sarah.

Scott grabbed his keys from the desk drawer, locked his office and walked out the door, forgetting to set the alarm. He called Sarah two more times before he even reached his car in the parking garage. He didn't leave additional messages, it would serve no purpose.

Scott called Sarah three more times during the thirty minute drive to her house. Where are you, he groaned as he hung up the phone after Sarah didn't answer. Again.

Sarah lived on the outskirts of town and expecting to be there in twenty minutes was only accomplished if one intended, in advance, to disobey speed limits and even a few stop signs. Scott sped down the road as quickly as possible and, yes, he even ran a few stop signs when the road was highly visible and he knew no one was coming from the other directions. Scott felt drained from the conversation with Dr. Patrick, but it wasn't about him. Everyone loved Janelle. She had a way of making herself at home in your life. This could not be happening to her. Although Sarah was older she was not the stronger sister. Scott found himself wishing Janelle was there to help her family with the news of her accident. The thought had him nervously chuckling at his rambling brain. What would her poor parents do when they found out? Thoughts continued to flood his brain as he drove. This was one of the longest drives he had ever made.

CHAPTER SEVEN

Dr. Patrick was finally going to go home. He had been at the hospital thirty-six hours straight. He needed to go home. He stopped in Janelle's room again one last time before he left the hospital. He had explained to the nursing staff again, in great detail and with very heartfelt emotion, Janelle could not be moved. At all. If Janelle woke up the nurses were instructed not to take that as a positive sign. He explained Janelle may not physically be in much pain. She would not be in much pain, but she was precariously close to death. After much discussion, Dr. Patrick was satisfied the nurses understood.

Logan was standing outside the ICU room, leaning against the wall, hat in his hand, head back against the wall, and his eyes closed. Dr. Patrick walked up to him. "Logan, shouldn't you be going home?"

Logan responded without moving his head or opening his eyes. "Seems neither of us want to leave her alone, Doc. Did you reach her family?" Logan opened his weary, bloodshot eyes and glanced over to where Dr. Patrick was standing.

"No, no, I didn't, but I did speak to her employer. I believe he is driving over to her sister's home and then they will call me. We are going to move her tomorrow to St. Joseph's in Phoenix. There is a doctor there who I believe will be able to best treat her." Dr. Patrick subconsciously knew he was violating several health information protection act rules, but he needed to tell Logan. The small town atmosphere won out for just this moment.

"Keep me posted, will ya' Doc?" Logan's tired voice sounded like he was begging.

The reality of disclosing information to Logan came from subconscious to an actual conscious thought. "Logan, you have no family ties at all to her, do you?"

"No. I just met her today. I think she needs someone to help her be strong and fight until she can be strong for herself. If her family wants me gone when they get here, I will go then. I don't want her to be all alone. She doesn't know anyone in Arizona from what she told Frank. If she wakes up, I may be the only familiar face she knows."

"Alright," the doctor responded, "until the family gets here to make decisions, I will consider you next friend for visitation purposes only." Both men nodded in understanding as Dr. Patrick walked in the room to see his patient before he left the hospital.

"Thanks, Doc." Logan watched him walk into her room and looked through the door as the doctor closed it behind him.

CHAPTER EIGHT

Sarah and Mitch spent the entire day together. Their breakfast ride turned into a trip to the aquarium, the mall, lunch, a movie and finally, a long walk and a wonderful dinner. After dinner Mitch took Sarah home.

"I'll walk you to the door," he said as he gently and affectionately bumped her forehead with his.

"Sounds good," she whispered smiling.

Mitch took Sarah's hand and brought their joined hands to his lips. He made eye contact with Sarah and gently kissed her clasped fingers. Sarah smiled and blushed.

He kissed her gently at the door, squeezed her hand he was still holding. Sarah sighed and squeezed his hand in return. Mitch let go of her hand and brushed a stray hair from her eyes. "I had an absolutely amazing day with you, Sarah." And without waiting for her to respond, he quickly turned and walked back to his car. Nothing more needed to be said and he knew he needed to leave before he changed his mind and invited himself inside her home. It had been a perfect day.

Sarah smiled after him. She had hoped he would come inside, but decided instantly it was perfect that he left the way he did. It was a perfect day, she whispered knowing he wouldn't hear her.

After Mitch waved from his car and drove away, Sarah stepped back inside the door she had been holding open. She glanced back one time at his tail lights as they drove away and smiled again. She was so excited about the day and so contented by Mitch's company. She felt like she could purr.

Sarah walked over near the couch, kicked off her boots and jeans and was just reaching for the blanket so she could snuggle under it on the couch when she realized she hadn't checked for messages. Sarah was waiting to hear from Janelle; the one promised "I arrived" phone all she had been able to convince Janelle to make.

Sarah walked over to the answering machine and smiled when she saw the light flashing. The flashing red digital read out on the machine bragged of six messages or missed calls. "Crazy Janelle," she giggled out loud "call and call all day when you know I had a date!"

Sarah pushed the play button and walked into the kitchen to get a glass of iced tea as the messages began to play.

"Beep. Ms. Beckett this is the Blood Bank calling to see if we can schedule your next donation. Please call us back at...," the call ended.

"Beep. Hi, this is Carl. I am trying to locate Steve. If this is his house, Steve, call me man."

"No, Steve here Carl, sorry," Sarah sang from the kitchen.

"Beep. Sarah, this is Scott Raskins. I need to speak to you as soon as possible. Please call my cell phone when you get this message. It's urgent."

"Oh no, no, no," said Sarah from the kitchen as she walked toward the answering machine. "My poor Jani hasn't been gone even one full day yet and you want to make her work. No way. Bu-bye Scott." She erased the message and moved on to the next.

Two hang ups and then another call from Scott that stopped Sarah cold.

"Beep. Sarah. This is Scott. Please, please call me immediately. You know what, never mind, I am almost at your house and I will wait for you there. There has been an accident. Janelle is, it is about Janelle. If you get this before I get here. Call me."

***

Sarah felt all the blood rush from her head and felt instantly lightheaded. She collapsed to her knees, "Oh God NO. God, no, no. Not Janelle!" She sobbed. Instinct must have kicked in because Sarah realized she had to dial Scott's number, no matter what he had to say.

Everything felt as if it was taking place in slow motion and through a thick haze she began to dial the phone. Sarah was white with fear and her shaking hands could barely hold still to press the numbers she needed. When the doorbell rang, Sarah could not distinguish it from the ringing phone.

Scott's voice mail answered immediately and Sarah hung up the phone thinking she must have dialed the wrong number. The doorbell rang again and this time it caught her attention. He's here, she said aloud, or at least she intended to. She walked quickly toward the door. It felt like a mile long walk.

When Sarah opened the door, Scott was standing there. "Is she dead? Please tell me she isn't dead." It was more of a prayer than a whispered conversation with Scott.

"Jani isn't dead, Sarah. It's bad, but she isn't dead." Just as he said the word dead the first time, Sarah started to sink at the knees. He had her in his arms holding her upright by the time he finished the sentence.

Scott realized Sarah must have just come home and started to get ready for bed because she was standing in his arms in a shirt, underwear and socks. He ushered her back into the house and closed the door behind them. Once inside he walked her to the couch and when she sat, he covered her with the blanket lying on the couch.

"Sarah, the doctor wants us to call him. He will explain everything to you. I will go with you to your parents and to Arizona if you want me to." She was crying and he never knew what to do with crying females. He just sat there next to her and let her gain her composure. How was she ever going to explain this to their parents? They would all be lost without Jani to get them through it. Jani was the strong one he had always thought to himself.

Sarah knew she was supposed to be doing something; something to help her sister. Everything was moving in slow motion. Sarah heard crying, but could not tell where it was coming from. All she knew is there was a large hole where the world was supposed to be and she physically ached at the thought of her sister dying. Sarah could not move or think clearly. The fear that Janelle might die, or be permanently gone, was too much. It seemed hours passed in the brief moments before she could focus. She moved out of Scott's arms and straightened the blanket across her lap only then realizing she had answered the door in her underwear. She tried to smile at him.

"Let's make the call. I will need to go see my parents. I will need to get to Arizona. I need to call work and tell them I am leaving. When do I tell them I will be back? What do I do, Scott?" She sounded like a scared child.

"We will take this one step at a time. Do you want to call the doctor from here, or from your parents' home?" Scott asked.

"Let's call now. I need to be able to tell my parents something. I should call Dad's doctor. I don't know how he'll handle this news." Sarah reached for the jeans she had discarded onto the floor and Scott politely found something else of interest in the room to stare at as Sarah stepped into the jeans and pulled them up. Dressed, she walked toward the phone in the kitchen. She picked it up and returned to Scott. Scott dialed Dr. Patrick's number from his cellphone. He dreaded this call. What if something had changed for the worst during the time he was driving? They had no idea what the doctor would say when he answered.

CHAPTER NINE

Sarah and her parents sat at the airport at 5:00 a.m. Monday morning waiting for Scott to get their boarding passes. Sarah was trying to make sense of what happened. She was trying to understand how Janelle could even have a decapitation. She had never heard such a thing. The doctor told them Janelle was dying unless they changed her current medical state.

Sarah tried the best she could to answer all of her parents' questions and to reassure them as much as possible. Her father was surprisingly strong and didn't need his doctor, nor did he have to take additional medication for his heart. He was being very protective of the women in his life. Scott had made all the arrangements for travel and a rental car at Sky Harbor Airport. His secretary was working on the hotel reservations and they would have the information upon their arrival. According to Scott, they should be with Janelle in four or five hours. Dr. Patrick had told Sarah that every minute mattered. Sarah could not believe that her sister was sitting in a strange city with no one to love her or be there while she was fighting for her very life.

Sarah hated Arizona.

Finally the three boarded the plane and were seated. Sarah's mother sat, hands in her lap, head bowed. Sarah knew she was praying. Her father had one hand on his wife's arm and his eyes were closed as he rested his head back against the headrest. Feeling confident her parents were okay for the time being, Sarah looked out the window. *Hang on Janelle, we are on our way.* Sarah thought to herself as the plane began to slowly taxi on the runway.

CHAPTER TEN

Janelle arrived safely at St. Joseph's Hospital and was immediately moved to intensive care. Dr. Curtis was there to greet her and a swarm of nurses went to work and gathered all the information they needed. Dr. Curtis was convinced, after his thorough examination of Janelle, she was a perfect candidate for the surgery. He knew her chances of survival were between slim and none. Dr. Curtis knew surgery was the only possible way to save her life. He believed Janelle would come out of her coma if they changed her medications. He wanted to speak with her to determine what she remembered and check her ability to respond. He also wanted her awake and conscious when her family was here. He wanted to be sure that everyone, including Janelle, if she responded as he expected, understood the risks. Mostly he knew that this might be the only opportunity that her family had to say goodbye to her and he wanted to afford them that chance. After stabilizing Janelle Dr. Curtis met with the nursing staff and gave them his instructions for the change in her medications. From what he had been told, her family should be here any time.

Dr. Curtis completed his rounds with his other surgical patients and studied Janelle's chart and the testing results. He went to check on Janelle before the family arrived. He would be the lead surgeon during the surgery and remain in charge of her care until the surgery was completed and he could get her through the first forty-eight hours after surgery.

As Dr. Curtis approached ICU there was a man sitting in the chair outside the door. He looked worried and tired as he stared down at the floor with his cowboy hat in his hands. Dr. Curtis wondered why no one had paged him to tell him Janelle's family had arrived.

"Hello." Dr. Curtis reached out his hand to shake the waiting man's hand as he rose to greet him. "I'm sorry I didn't come sooner, I wasn't aware you had arrived. I am the surgeon who will be caring for Janelle and performing the surgery if it is agreed to be in her best interests. My name is Dr. Curtis."

"Pleased to meet you Doc, I'm Logan. I didn't tell anyone to send for you. I just knew Janelle had been transported down here from Flagstaff and I came to the ICU floor. When do you expect to make a decision about the surgery?"

Dr. Patrick explained briefly what would happen. Logan spoke intently to the doctor. Logan knew answers from the doctor would make him feel like someone was in control. Dr. Patrick knew patient's families always felt better when they knew what would be happening to their loved one.

"Well, as soon as the rest of your family arrives I will explain the procedure and the risks to everyone. I want to be able to explain it all to Janelle also. I expect that she will be awake soon. I have taken her off of the medications that kept her in the induced coma. Would you like to see her for a moment?" Dr. Curtis asked.

Logan knew he should tell the doctor that he was not her family, but no one was here and he had to see her. He had to tell her to be strong and that someone cared. "I would love to see her for a moment. Thank you Doc."

Logan tried hard not to gasp as he walked in. She looked so tiny lying in the bed, hooked up to monitors; I.V. and oxygen. The Halo Brace around her head that held her together and kept her alive looked like a cage. The doctor checked the chart and checked the monitors and walked out the door. He seemed to be leaving Logan a moment with Janelle.

Logan pulled the chair close to the bed. He reached over to touch her arm, but fear of hurting her stopped him. Instead he rested his hand next to hers. "Hey Janelle. It's Logan. You're a trooper, quite a feisty little lass my dad would say if he met you. Hold on and concentrate on being well. The next couple of days will be tough, but you're strong and I could tell by your face when I watched you at Shannon's Luck that you have determination. I'll be here for you. Your sister and folks will be here anytime. Everything is going to be fine. Keep telling yourself that and believe it, okay?" He had leaned over and was talking softly very near to her ear; his voice barely a whisper. Logan looked at her, she didn't move. He knew she could hear him. She simply had to hear him.

Suddenly Janelle's machines began beeping and Logan knew something was terribly wrong. He saw the heart rate monitor dropping and the blood pressure reading dropping too. *Oh God...* Logan almost shouted as he turned to the door and saw Dr. Curtis and two nurses already hurrying through the door.

"I'm afraid you will have to leave her now," Dr. Curtis dictated as he approached.

Logan kissed Janelle's cheek. "I'll be here for you, keep fighting." Then Logan complied willingly with the doctor and quickly left the room. Logan would sit outside the room and wait to see her again, at least until the family arrived. They may very well not appreciate his presence, but if whatever was going on in that room didn't turn in her favor, they may very well need him there.

CHAPTER ELEVEN

Janelle felt herself lying under what felt like a rock. Her head hurt and she could hear someone talking. Something didn't seem right, but she couldn't put her finger on what it could be.

Janelle opened her eyes and squeezed them shut and then opened and shut them again a time or two to clear the blurriness away and hopefully bring everything into focus. *Wow*, she thought to herself, *I certainly feel the effects of whatever I was drinking.* Her head was pounding.

Janelle stood up and looked around. *Oh no, something is so not right*, she said out loud. As Janelle looked out over the tall grassy field she realized what she saw before her came from a photo she had seen of castles in Ireland. For some reason, though, the castle didn't look like it had gone to ruin as it did in the photograph she had seen. She also knew she must be dreaming.

Well, Janelle, she announced to no one there, *if you are going to have a dream about a time travel adventure, try to find a gorgeous rogue like you always read about.*

Janelle decided to go with the dream. She walked down the dirt path toward a tall rock wall that surrounded the hill the castle sat on. She thought she saw a man shoeing a horse, but when she looked again, he was gone. Janelle walked to where she had seen him standing, but no one was there and no one appeared again.

In the distance Janelle heard a man yelling, but she didn't see anyone. She wondered what was going on. Janelle was conscious of the fact she was dreaming, but she somehow wouldn't wake up. She heard the man talking loudly again. She heard him say his name was Shannon. He sounded like he was flirting with someone, but no one was anywhere to be seen.

Janelle snickered to herself while standing firmly with feet slightly parted and hands on her hips. She could not figure out where this dream was going and why she couldn't see the people she could hear.

Suddenly Janelle heard someone say her name. She turned quickly to look back where she had come from, but she didn't see anyone.

"Be strong, Janelle." It was a man's voice she heard, but it was not the same man she heard flirting with the woman. It didn't really matter because Janelle couldn't see anyone.

Janelle was starting to get frustrated. At that very moment she felt someone grabbed her from behind and she felt herself being dragged backwards. She tried to cry out, but her voice no longer had sound. Janelle tried to kick free, but her arms and legs wouldn't move. She heard speaking again, but now she couldn't make out the exact words being spoken. Janelle tried to remember the name of the man she heard earlier. She wanted to cry out for help. Shannon, it was Shannon, she was glad she remembered it and wondered where he was. She wondered if he would hear her. Janelle felt herself being pulled backwards again and cried out.

"Help me, Shannon," she screamed, but she was pretty sure no sound came out of her mouth. There was no way he would hear her. Janelle had no idea what was happening and she panicked. Something was terribly wrong. "Help me, Shannon, please help me," she screamed, but again no words left her mouth. She fought as hard as she could, but something was holding her head and her arms and she could not move or see what was holding her. Everything was going black. Janelle heard the man speak again, "You are a strong one little lass, a feisty lass my Dad would say. I'll be here for you, keep fighting."

Fighting? What am I fighting? What is going on? Why is he saying he'll help me, but isn't doing anything? Janelle all of a sudden felt she couldn't breathe. She knew something was terribly wrong and Janelle wanted very much to wake up. She willed herself to leave this crazy dream, but could not awaken. In her fight, she cried, she felt afraid of the unseen force that held her down and afraid of why she was in this strange place to begin with. If this truly was a dream, why wasn't she waking up? Reality was fading and she felt herself drifting.

"Please help me, Shannon, please help me," Janelle mumbled over and over hoping he would hear. She felt his hand touch her face and she realized she couldn't even see this man. She tried to reach out to him, but Janelle couldn't move her arms. Then she felt a kiss on her cheek, but she couldn't respond. Then, she felt...nothing. Everything went black. The dream had finally ended.

Janelle was unaware of the medical team assembling quickly in her room. Janelle was unaware her life hung precariously in the balance. Janelle was unaware she wasn't sleeping, but in an induced coma. Janelle wasn't aware a real, living and breathing man had sat at her bedside, encouraging her and willing her to live.

As quickly as Janelle's condition had begun to plummet, it returned to normal. The doctor ordered no visitors permitted in her room until the rest of her family arrived and decisions would be made. Satisfied Janelle was stable for now, Dr. Curtis left the room to advise Logan he would not be able to see Janelle until the rest of his family arrived. Janelle remained unaware of all of this.

CHAPTER TWELVE

Sarah and her parents finally found the hospital and raced to the fifth floor where Janelle was being cared for. They exited the elevator and approached the ICU Nurse's Station. Sarah spoke for the family, "We are the Beckett's. Janelle Beckett's family."

Dr. Curtis was at a computer entering notes. He stood and greeted Sarah and Mr. & Mrs. Beckett. "Hello, I am Dr. Curtis. I am attending Janelle."

"Can we see her now, please?" Mrs. Beckett asked, half-controlled tears flowing down her plump face, her voice shaking with fear. Her eyes were red and it was obvious she'd been crying long before arriving at the hospital. Her short grey hair was messy and she looked exhausted

"I know you want to see her and you will. I would like to speak with you about her condition before we go into her room. Come with me, please, let's talk in private." Dr. Curtis grabbed the computer so he could read from Janelle's electronic chart and led the way to a consultation room. The Beckett's followed.

They sat in his office and discussed everything Janelle

had been through. Each of her injuries were explained, including exactly what happens when someone sustains an internal decapitation. All questions they fired at Dr. Curtis were answered with as much certainty as he could provide. He explained that Janelle was a miracle at this moment by even having fought this far to stay alive. He allowed them time to shed their tears. He could tell grief was a cold hand over each of their hearts and they were feeling the overwhelming hopelessness of the situation.

"I need to also let you know we had a scare with Janelle about an hour ago. Her vitals all seemed to crash at the same time. It returned to normal as quickly as it occurred. The reason I am telling you this is that I don't think you have much time to make a decision on where we go from here. Janelle is, well, she may look fine to you when you see her, she may be speaking and not feeling as pained as she should feel, but please don't misunderstand what you don't see and don't hear from her. I have to tell you, Janelle is dying right now and we need to change that." Dr. Curtis knew the words were harsh, but he needed the family to shock back to decision making and process their grief later.

Mr. & Mrs. Beckett began sobbing at the same moment. How could their baby be dying? Children were supposed to bury their parents, not the other way around. Sarah kneeled before her huddled parents and hugged them both. She cooed soothingly trying to help them calm down. Decisions needed to be made and Sarah wanted them to get made soon. She knew Janelle's life was hanging by a thread. She just had no idea how to make her parents come to terms quickly with the possible loss of their daughter.

"Please remember, this can be done." Dr. Curtis' voice conveyed his deep rooted belief that this surgery was meant to be and was meant to be for Janelle. "I know we can help her if the swelling has decreased. Janelle should be awake soon. I want her to be able to participate in this decision if at all possible. I also want to talk with her to be sure she has no signs of any brain damage from the accident. I need the three of you, and her brother, to make that final decision."

"Her brother?" Mr. Beckett looked confused. "We don't have a son." His voice was barely a whisper. "We only have our precious daughters." Mr. & Mrs. Beckett broke again into quiet racking tears.

Dr. Curtis didn't want to press. He knew they would recognize the man when they saw him. Maybe he was a cousin, it wasn't worth pushing right now.

"Let's go see Janelle, if you are ready." Dr. Curtis announced. They were ready. At least they thought they were ready.

As they approached Janelle's ICU room the man was still sitting by the room waiting to hear word or see Janelle. Dr. Curtis realized that Janelle's family did not greet the waiting man. He chalked it up to grief and went to check on Janelle. He expected they would soon realize Logan was sitting there waiting for them. Dr. Curtis went into Janelle's room first to check her status.

Logan approached Janelle's family. "You must be Sarah and Janelle's folks." He extended his hand to shake Mr. Beckett's hand. Mr. Beckett reached his shaking hand out and shook hands with Logan.

Mrs. Beckett stared thinking he must somehow know Janelle. "I am afraid we do not know you, Sir," Janelle's frail mother announced with a small shaking voice. "How do you know our Jani?"

Logan smiled and told the crib note version of Janelle

coming to Shannon's Luck and explained that he had followed her to be sure she arrived at the Mendoza cabin and he had seen the accident. He knew she had no family in Flagstaff or Phoenix. Logan explained he simply couldn't leave her there alone until they all arrived.

"You know Janelle better than I do, you know how she "grabs" your heart." Logan almost sounded apologetic. "I just wanted to be sure she wasn't alone. I just wanted to give her an anchor, you know a voice she might recognize telling her to keep fighting. I just wanted her to have someone to believe in her until you got here. I can leave now, I really don't want to intrude." Logan didn't usually talk that much and he certainly revealed more emotion than he was comfortable with. He looked down at his hat as he turned it round and round by the brim. He suddenly felt very much like an intruder.

Mrs. Beckett and Sarah hugged him at the exact same moment and began to cry. What a wonderful gift this man was to be there and to care. They both thanked him and asked that he stay while they went in to see Janelle. Sarah explained Dr. Curtis' treatment plan, as he had explained it to them. She talked of the risks of the surgery and how they had no other option. Logan knew the things she was telling him as he had been kept remarkably informed in their absence, but he knew that the words being said out loud were cathartic to Sarah and needed to be said. Explaining to Logan what she knew was a small element of control for her.

Dr. Curtis came out of Sarah's room smiling. "She is awake. She can't respond and she is groggy. As she wakes more she may become afraid and agitated. She has no idea she was even in an accident and may have a rush of overwhelming emotion. She may also not know you. You have to be prepared for anything. I have to ask you to control your reactions. No matter what happens. We can't risk upsetting her. I hate to say this to you, but you need to remember, as Janelle lies in that hospital bed, she may appear to be doing okay, but as I told you in my office...," the doctor paused. He hated having to be so harsh with family, but they could make or break a patient's recovery. "But, you need to remember, she is hanging on by a thread until I am able to operate. She can't move, not even slightly. No hugging, no touching, no bed sitting. Just respond to her lead. Ready?" What a question that was after the speech he had just delivered. The looks on their faces told him the family understood the gravity of the situation.

Logan saw Mr. Beckett tightly grasp his wife's hand. He reached over and took Sarah's. She was white with fear. "Come on, Sarah." He gently tugged her hand as he held it firmly in his and began to lead her into Janelle's room. Her parents would go in together after Sarah and Logan.

Sarah walked up beside the bed and realized that she had to almost lean in so Janelle could see her. Her eyes were open and appeared glazed over with terror.

"Hi Baby Sister. You're okay. You're okay. Don't be afraid. Just rest. Logan is with me." Sarah pointed to Logan as she spoke.

The look in Janelle's eyes as they darted between Sarah and Logan bordered on terror. It was clear she did not recognize either of them. Dr. Curtis approached and spoke, taking control of the situation to calm Janelle.

"Janelle, I'm Dr. Curtis. If you can understand me, blink your eyes two times."

Tears welled up in Janelle's eyes. She blinked two times.

"Good. Good, Janelle. Do you recognize your sister and

Logan?" Dr. Curtis continued.

***

Janelle knew she should recognize this man. She knew it, but she couldn't remember him. Logan was looking at her with so much emotion in his eyes that she had to blink two times to reassure both Logan and Sarah she knew them. At least she knew Sarah. Janelle blinked two times.

"Janelle. You were involved in a very severe car accident on Sunday evening in Flagstaff. You are currently at the hospital in Phoenix. Do you understand me so far?"

Janelle blinked two times and her lower lip quivered, tears began to fall from the sides of her eyes, just as she closed them.

"Good. You're okay. Just take a breath. I want you to know where you are medically. Do you understand?"

Janelle opened her teary eyes and blinked twice, without making eye contact with anyone.

Dr. Curtis continued, "You have a severe head and spinal injury which require surgery. It isn't a brain injury, more of a spinal injury. Surgery is your only option, Janelle. And the surgery needs to occur very soon. Do you understand?"

She opened her eyes that were pooled with her tears and blinked twice. Tears spilled out and down the sides of her face.

"Do you want to proceed with the surgery or do you want your family to make that decision?"

Janelle looked at Sarah and stared. She closed her eyes after a few minutes. She did not open them again. Janelle knew that if she just kept them closed this nightmare would be over. She also knew in her heart that her sister would take care of her.

"Let's leave her now and let your parents come in briefly. After that we'll make the decision."

CHAPTER THIRTEEN

The surgical procedure took three and a half hours. During this time a small incision was made in the back of Janelle's neck. She remained in the halo brace during the entire surgery. Holes were drilled through the first vertebrae and the cranium. Guide wires were used to pull everything into alignment. Two titanium screws were inserted diagonally from each side of the first vertebrae to the cranium. The screws bit perfectly into the bone and felt tightly fitted. A piece of bone from Janelle's pelvis was placed over each set of screws and wired into place over the junction of the spine and cranium. For this surgery to be a success the bone had to grow. The screws were only a brace to hold everything in place while she healed. The bone graft was the key. It had worked before. Dr. Curtis was counting on it working again. He was pleased with the outcome of the surgery.

Dr. Curtis would wait for Janelle to awaken from the anesthesia to see if there was any paralysis or brain damage and then she had to go back into an induced coma. He would explain to her family that this was necessary for a week due to the fact that a sleeping brain uses less blood and therefore creates less swelling. Janelle needed every advantage she could get. She had a long road ahead of her. Dr. Curtis could not wait to tell the family that she had survived the surgery and could begin that long road to recovery.

Dr. Curtis walked out of the surgical room. The Beckett family, and Logan, met him a few steps outside of the operating room. "She is a fighter," he said smiling. "Surgery went well. I am counting on the bone graft to take. It will be months before we know the level of her recovery, but it starts today."

Dr. Curtis went on to explain that she would be allowed to awaken briefly. Janelle would be put through a short series of tests to see if there was any paralysis, nerve or cognitive damage. The family handled the news as well as could be expected when told she would be placed back into an induced coma and that Janelle's hospital stay was expected to be several weeks before she could go to a rehabilitation location.

Everyone thanked the doctor and hugs were passed around freely. Many happy tears were being shed in that waiting room. Dr. Curtis loved being able to give good news. No matter what tomorrow brought, for now Janelle had a fighting chance and to be able to tell the family that fact made his day. The family knew they wouldn't be able to see Janelle the rest of the day. Dr. Curtis told them to make sure they got something to eat and then rested well. He reassured Mr. Beckett he would contact them at the slightest change and asked that they please go take care of themselves. They reluctantly agreed, but wanted to be back so they were there for her later that day. She was expected to awake after dinner. They would be here. They all understood the long recovery road, but where there was life there was hope and Janelle was definitely alive.

"Well, do you want me to help you get to your hotel?" Logan asked.

"We are staying walking distance from here, Logan. Thank you, though," Mr. Beckett said appreciatively. Secretly he was glad to be able to walk off a little of the pent up energy he had stored waiting on the news of Janelle's surgery.

"Well, I am going to head to my hotel. I have been here since they brought her yesterday and I am just rather tired. I also need to let my family know where I am. I left rather quickly and they may think I have gone off the deep end or something if I don't call. I left my number with the nurse. It's to my cell phone. Please call me if there are any changes. I will stop back by later this evening when she is awake if it is okay with you." Logan smiled, a slow smile that was based in fear for Janelle, fatigue and something that was deeper.

Mrs. Beckett reached for Logan's cheek and he lowered to her. She kissed him on the other cheek and told him with her gentlest voice "You are welcome here always my son."

"Thank you. I am so relieved the surgery went well. She will have a battle ahead, but I already know she's a feisty lass and will fight hard," Logan stated with authority he hoped gave the family hope.

"Thank you, Logan," Sarah said and reached over to touch his shoulder. "Sleep well and we'll see you tomorrow."

"Yes, tomorrow." Logan smiled and nodded his head as he turned to walk towards the elevator. The family lingered briefly. He expected it was very difficult for them to leave their daughter alone in the hospital knowing she was still fighting for her life.

CHAPTER FOURTEEN

Logan checked in to his hotel. When Logan got back to his room he saw his cell phone on the dresser and realized he had forgotten it when he went to the hospital. Logan picked up his phone and saw he had several missed calls and several messages. He called his voice mail, entered his code and listened half-heartedly. The first message almost stopped his heart. It was Kelly, his father suffered a heart attack earlier that day. He wasn't expected to survive the attack. She had called him several time over a four hour period. He was afraid to listen to the rest of the messages and opted for calling Kelly instead.

God, don't let him die. Not at all and especially with me in Phoenix. Logan prayed out loud as he dialed Kelly's number.

Kelly answered on the first ring just as he expected she would. Before she could even say 'hello' Logan spoke, "I am on my way home." As he spoke he grabbed his duffle bag and threw it over his shoulder. He was grateful he hadn't unpacked it earlier that day. "Is he still alive, Kelly?"

"Barely Logan, please hurry," was Kelly's tearful response. "I have been trying to call you for hours. I called and called, Logan. I went by the house, and Dad's place. Where are you?" Kelly's voice was breaking and Logan knew she was doing everything she could not to sob into the phone.

"I'll explain when I get there Kelly, it won't make sense to you if I try now. Unfortunately I'm driving from Phoenix. I'll be there as quickly as I can and I'm going straight to the hospital. I love you and I'll see you in a few hours. I'm sorry, Kelly, I will get there as quickly as I can." Logan hung up so he could get in the car and get to Flagstaff.

As he hung up he heard Kelly say "please drive safe, Logan." Logan didn't intend to be rude when he hung up on Kelly as she was still speaking, he was just so caught in the emotion of yet another tragedy. This was his father. He couldn't die. His father was a rock of a man. He had lived a hardworking and tough life, especially after Logan's mother died. Logan's younger brother, Patrick always made life hard for them all. Logan knew he didn't have time to get into the whole thought process about his brother and his untimely death, nor the pain he caused Dad, Logan or Kelly and the baby. He shook the thought out of his head and thought of his Dad and willed him to live.

Logan realized he hadn't checked out of the hotel and called them first to explain the emergency and that he was checking out. Then he called Sarah's cellphone. As he expected, it went straight to voicemail. He left a message there had been a family emergency. He would be in touch when he could and to call him if anything changed, or even just to update him in the morning after they spoke to the doctor. He promised to return her call as soon as he could.

Logan was soon on the highway headed north toward Flagstaff. *Hang on, Dad. Please hang on.*

CHAPTER FIFTEEN

Janelle awoke to someone pinching her foot. She still could feel that force holding her down.

Someone spoke. "Can you feel that Janelle? Can you feel me pinching your toe?"

"Yes, I can," she rasped realizing her throat was sore, "What happened?"

"You had surgery Janelle," the nurse stated. "Your family is outside. I'll get the doctor. He will bring in your family."

***

Dr. Curtis had been writing up chart notes at the nurses' station just outside Janelle's room and got up and walked quickly to her room when he heard the nurse say she would get the doctor.

Dr. Curtis walked quickly into the room and smiled at Janelle when he saw her eyes were open. You are quite the trooper Miss Beckett. Allow me to introduce myself again, I'm Dr. Curtis, your surgeon. How are you feeling right now?" He asked.

"Sore, scared and confused." Janelle's eyes welled up with tears again.

That's actually good, he thought to himself knowing it meant she was aware of her surroundings. "Ok, ok," he patted her arm. "Let's start from the beginning."

Dr. Curtis went through the drill of cognitive exercises regarding her name, address, date, where she was, etc. He was confident in her responses and pleased that it appeared she didn't have any issues from the surgery. Dr. Curtis spent a very long time explaining what had happened, her stay in the Flagstaff hospital, the procedure she had undergone and what the recovery expectations were. Janelle wept silently when she was told she would be put back into a coma for a couple more weeks. The thought filled her with dread.

"So, am I out of the woods or am I going to die?" Janelle's voice was timid. "Will I come out of the induced coma?" She whispered afraid of the answers.

"Janelle," he touched her arm again smiling at how brave she was acting when he could tell she wanted to fall apart. "You are not going to die while you are in the induced coma. The purpose is to allow your brain to rest and reduce all swelling. We are counting on the graft to take and it will protect and strengthen your skull and spine. I can't guarantee the prognosis of your recovery. I do know you have survived the worst part. We have to be very patient to see your level of recovery." Dr. Curtis didn't give false hope or overstate what he expected for recovery. He would rather be careful with his words than have to apologize later. But, if he had anything to say about it, Janelle was not only going to survive, but thrive and live a long and happy life.

Janelle thought she nodded, not yet realizing the halo

brace made it impossible for her to do so. "Can I see my family, please," she stated trying to block out the fear that was growing in her head.

Dr. Curtis didn't feel the need to respond. He realized the determination in her voice. He knew she was finished speaking with him and needed to process their conversation and what he had told her. She would have to work through it in her own time. Dr. Curtis knew he couldn't help her with that. "Nurse, send in her family, please," he said to the nurse outside Janelle's room as he walked towards the door. "Janelle, I will be back to see you after your family leaves."

Janelle knew what that meant even if he didn't say it and she began to cry. She couldn't help it. Everything felt hopeless and she felt trapped. Her mother and father walked into her room at that exact moment. They saw tears falling down her cheeks even though her eyes were closed.

"Baby," her mother said and quickly moved to the bedside. She reached for Janelle's hand. "Talk to me Jani. Talk to me."

Janelle could not handle hearing her mother's voice when she felt so emotionally fragile. As her father also sat at her bedside and she saw the look of concern on his face, Janelle started sobbing.

"I am so sorry, Mom. So sorry, Daddy," she cried wishing that they could hold her tight against their chest instead of just holding her hand. "I can't help it, I just can't help it." Her voice broke and the sobs racked her body.

Her parent whispered hope in unison and cooed at her, reassuring her everything would be fine.

"Janelle, Mom and I are going nowhere until we can

take you home with us."

"Oh, Daddy." Janelle tried to stop crying, but her tears were one more thing she had no control over.

When their fifteen minutes were up they had to leave the room. Sarah was given a brief visit with her sister before Dr. Curtis returned to the room.

While she waited for her sister, Janelle tried to calm down.

"Hi Sis," Sarah sung to her as she walked into the hospital room. Sarah had vowed to take the light hearted "everything is fine" approach to her visit. "So, guess you weren't in town long when you found that gorgeous cowboy, huh?" She smiled at Janelle.

Janelle's confusion was apparent. "Who are you talking about, Sarah?"

"Logan, Logan who's been here with you since you got here. Logan that you met at the restaurant in Flagstaff. Logan, the tall handsome guy. With a hat. Did you already know him, is that why you picked Arizona?" Sarah teased slightly and smiled with a joy she didn't feel. She hoped the slight teasing would bring out her sister's smile Sarah longed to see.

"I don't know him, Sarah. I don't think I have ever seen him before. I know I should know him and that scares me. I don't even remember arriving in Flagstaff and I don't remember the accident. I only know I saw the sign for Flagstaff and now I am here." Janelle was crying again. She so desperately needed someone to help her remember what happened and knew she could trust Sarah with her tears and with the truth about what Janelle knew and didn't know.

"Never mind. Never mind. I'm sorry. I didn't mean to upset you. I love you, Janelle. We'll figure it out when you are a little better, ok? Scott sends his best. He was the one the hospital contacted first. He is going to come out and see you when he can, when you are up to it." Sarah rubbed Janelle's arm as she talked, it was the closest to a hug she could manage.

Janelle closed her eyes and took a deep breath. She just wanted life to be back to normal. "How was your date, Sarah? The horseback ride?" Janelle kept her eyes closed as she spoke quietly.

At that very moment Sarah realized she had been gone two days and had never told Mitch what was going on. Sarah made a mental note to call him when she left visiting her sister.

"It was perfect. I will tell you all about it over a latte when you are better, deal?"

"Deal, Sarah. I love you." Janelle squeezed Sarah's hand. "Tell Mom and Daddy I will be fine, ok. Take care of them. If anything happens to me, Sarah. If I...," she trailed off. "Well, you know where my papers are, right? And you know I love you, right."

Sarah was overcome by emotion and the lump in her throat made it impossible for her to respond. Sarah was bombarded with the overwhelming fear Janelle would die and gratitude for having a sister who loved her family so much she made knowing how to sort out her affairs a priority. Janelle was fighting for her life, but still thinking of her family.

Before Sarah could even respond, Dr. Curtis and a nurse walked in. Sarah had to leave and they stayed in the room with her.

It was going to be a long two weeks.

CHAPTER SIXTEEN

Sarah called Mitch when she returned to the hotel. Sarah explained everything and how she was staying in Phoenix as long as Janelle needed her. Mitch agreed to watch her cat and said he would come out on Friday to spend the weekend with her at the hospital. At that moment Sarah realized she loved him. She believed Mitch loved her. Why he was put into her life at that moment was a mysterious gift Sarah did not intend to question.

The next call Sarah made was to her supervisor to explain what had happened with her sister. Her employer understood her immediate leave of absence. She had several weeks of vacation and sick leave, there was no problem about loss of pay. Her supervisor told Sarah to take as long as she needed and wished healing for Janelle.

Sarah took a shower and cried until the water ran cold. She knew her parents were in the next room doing the same thing. They each needed time to deal with the grief, the fear, and the events that had changed their lives.

CHAPTER SEVENTEEN

Logan's father passed away. The funeral was to be that weekend. Kelly held him close as he cried. Little Jake was only three and didn't understand why all the grownups were crying and it scared him. Jake cried because the people who made everything okay in his world were crying and not because of an understanding of what had happened to his grandfather.

Kelly had tried to explain that "Papa" was gone to heaven. He still didn't understand and Jake told his crying mother not to worry, his Papa would tell him later. It would be a secret until then.

"Logan," Kelly whispered, "Let's go home. We can figure out what to do from there."

Logan, Kelly and Jake went to Dad's home. Logan found his Dad's personal papers right where he had been told they would be. Logan set the papers on the desk and stared at them. He would read them tomorrow and start making arrangements then. Today he had nothing left.

Kelly put Jake to bed while Logan called the hospital and found that Janelle had woken up, she seemed fine and that she was to be in an induced coma for several days or so. He knew that Sarah and the family would be distraught. Janelle was alive, his dad was dead. This had been too trying a week. Logan went to his dad's desk and brought out a bottle of bourbon. He first lit a fire and then grabbed a shot glass for his bourbon. When Kelly came downstairs Logan had already poured himself a few drinks. As soon as she sat down, Logan started telling her about Janelle. He talked for over an hour and he pulled back shots of bourbon. Logan told Kelly he knew Janelle belonged to him and she couldn't die too. Then he hung his head in his hands and cried. Kelly knew it was the bourbon talking and when Logan fell asleep in the recliner, she took the bottle and the shot glass from him and covered him with a blanket.

***

The funeral would be on Friday. Logan was so tired of burying people he loved. First his Ma, then Patrick who made awful choices and whose drug addicted lifestyle caused him to drive his car off a winding road, leaving the family, Kelly and Jake with no one. Logan had known from the time Patrick was a troubled teenager he was going to cause his own demise. It didn't make it any easier when it actually happened. Despite all the efforts made, drugs were a ghost that haunted Patrick. They finally got what they wanted. They ended his life. Logan felt great guilt when Patrick died because a wave of relief crossed him. Relief that he no longer had to wonder when it would happen. Relief that he had walked out on Dad, Logan, Kelly and Jake months before it happened. Relief that Kelly and Jake, or Dad, weren't in the car with him. His grief and regret with his dad's passing were different.

Logan knew he was going to get through this week with Kelly and then take a drive. He would go to Phoenix to see

Janelle, to touch life for a while.

***

The funeral was rough. Everyone they knew was there. Little Jake finally understood when he saw the casket and had hung on to Logan all day crying. Kelly, who had no other family now in Flagstaff, except Logan and Jake, couldn't bring herself to see Dad in the casket. The hour long funeral and burial that came after seemed to take days.

***

After the funeral, Kelly approached Logan. "Logan, where am I going to go? Patrick left me in such debt, I have nothing left. If I have to move from Dad's I don't know where I will go." She sounded like a lost child. "You know my circumstances. I can't go back to Michigan. My mother is probably still not speaking to me."

"Honey," Logan took her in his arms and cooed at her, "You aren't going anywhere. Shannon's Luck is your home. If you don't feel comfortable there, move in my place. It is plenty big enough. It also makes the most sense. I need to be there for Jake. He is going to really need mearound now, with his dad and Papa gone. I plan on being there for both of you, understand?"

"I love you Logan, why didn't I pick you instead of Patrick?" She half smiled.

"I am a better brother-in-law than I would be a husband, Kelly. I was way too busy for a family of my own when you came around. You were ready to be attached to someone, I would have hurt you for sure. Besides, there will be another man for you out there someday and then I will still be here to turn to for advice."

"Kelly," he continued. "Drive with me in the morning to Phoenix. I want to see Janelle and her family. I want you to come with me."

Kelly nodded. What was his obsession with this woman? The only obsession she had ever known Logan to have was his hatred for Mr. Mendoza's daughter, Rachel. Everyone hated Rachel. For luring Patrick from his last rehab efforts with drugs, sex, money and fast cars. Kelly shook her head and decided not to go down that path. She could barely maintain civility toward that woman and right now was not the time to tend that wound.

CHAPTER EIGHTEEN

It was Sunday morning, again. Janelle had been moved out of the ICU, but remained on the critical care floor. Logan, Kelly and Jake came to the hospital. Kelly and Jake waited in the lobby while Logan was let in to see her. He visited a short while and Logan realized he was at peace sitting beside her. He brushed her cheek with his hand and felt her warmth underneath his hand. She was alive and he inhaled and exhaled his first truly deep breath since she was in the accident. She was alive. Logan's eyes filled with tears. He knew they were for the loss of his father. He knew sitting here by Janelle was the only place he felt complete right now.

"I'm here, Janelle, I'm here. Keep fighting for me, okay." He gently ran his hand along her arm, careful not to bump the countless needles or wires coming out of her arm.

He regretted not seeing any of Janelle's family, but he knew Kelly wanted to get back to Flagstaff. They had a lot of business to take care of and she only went with Logan out of fear he would not come back to Flagstaff.

Logan left a note for Sarah so she would know he had

been there and he asked her to please call him. Logan also added he wanted to explain his absence all week, but preferred to talk to her than write a note. He didn't want to write the words stating his father had died and he didn't want anything about death in Janelle's room.

As Logan was leaving the hospital Sarah saw him leaving. At first she wasn't sure it was him and he was too far to call out. Sarah realized it actually was Logan and then she a small child in his arms and him holding hands with the blonde walking beside him.

Sarah was slightly shocked and a little irritated. *Apparently Logan has a wife and child,* Sarah said as a matter of fact statement to herself. Not that it really mattered. Logan had never told the family he wasn't married, he just acted as if Janelle were somehow special to him as more than a friend. *Oh well,* she said out loud and shrugged, *it doesn't matter. We'll be leaving here soon."*

Logan forgotten, Sarah went into Janelle's room and sat with her sister for a couple hours until her parents came. It was the same routine every day. Mom and Dad would sit with Janelle through dinner time after Sarah had spent the afternoon. This allowed their parents to rest in the afternoon. Last thing Sarah needed was a bad health turn with either of her parent's health. Sarah read to Janelle. She found silly books from their childhood in the library in the children's ward. Sarah didn't know if Janelle could even hear her. Sarah knew the reading was more for herself than for Janelle. Sarah hoped Janelle could hear her and hoped the books and conversations she had eased Janelle's mind as she healed.

"Oh Janelle," Sarah stopped reading the book she had been reading, "I didn't tell you Mitch is coming in to town this evening. It's Friday. Mitch told me this morning he decided to take a couple vacation days and is going to stay until Thursday. He will probably come to see you tomorrow. Tonight I am going to probably go to dinner with him. I hope you don't think that's wrong, with you being here and all. I just need to be away from the hotel and I am so relieved he is here. I can't wait until you can open your eyes and are back here with us. Soon, they tell us. You are doing remarkable. The doctor seems very pleased with everything he sees on the MRI and the x-rays are showing healing. You are so strong Janelle. You are such a fighter. I'm so very proud of you. I have a secret to tell you." Sarah just talked and talked. She leaned down and placed a hand on Janelle's shoulder. "I love Mitch, Janelle. It hasn't been that long, I know. You probably think I'm crazy, but I just feel I love him. If you think that's crazy, I think he loves me too. I don't know if it is everything you are going through that makes us more aware of everything, but I just love him. I want him here so badly. I want him to be here for me and for you and for Mom and Dad. I just want him here. Oh, Janelle, I so need to hear what you think of all this. Soon you can tell me. Soon, Baby Sister." Sarah maneuvered a gentle kiss on Janelle's cheek and wiped away the tears that were spilling over her cheeks. She needed her sister back and seeing her lying in the hospital bed, in a halo brace, with wires and tubes everywhere broke Sarah's heart.

Mr. & Mrs. Beckett arrived and talked with Sarah about the afternoon. They were pleased that her friend Mitch was coming. She seemed so excited about it and they both knew she needed someone to be there just for her. After reassuring her parents Janelle had been fine all afternoon, Sarah prepared to leave.

"Sarah, we want you to enjoy your dinner with your

friend tonight. You have been so devoted sitting here day in and day out. You probably need an evening off. If anything changes, we will call your cell phone. Don't come back here this evening after your dinner, okay?" Her dad held her chin in his hand gently as he looked into her sad weary eyes.

"Dad," Sarah began. "I will..."

"No, Sarah. You are no good to anyone if you don't take care of yourself. Janelle would want you to continue to live your life. Go out to dinner, maybe a movie, maybe talk to your friend about all the things you won't say to us. We have each other to confide in. You are keeping this all inside being strong for everyone. Go out. Don't come back here and don't call here tonight unless we call you first. I love you and so does your mother and your sister. Go." Dad was firm, yet loving in his words.

Sarah stared at her dad, torn about what to do.

"Listen to your father, Baby," her mom said quietly.

Sarah hugged her parents and left for the hotel to shower and change.

***.

The taxi arrived to take Sarah to the airport. Mitch would be here soon. Sarah was so excited to see him. She wore a fitted denim skirt that hit about mid-calf. It was really warm out so Sarah chose a frilly tank top that she thought really flattered her figure. She hoped it caught Mitch's attention and made him glad he flew to Arizona to see her.

***

Finally Mitch's plane arrived. Sarah waited outside the restricted area and watched everyone arrive. The people were smiling and excited to see their friends and family.

"Mitch!" Sarah ran toward him as she saw him walk out of the restricted hall from the gate.

Mitch dropped his bags and drew her tightly into his arms. He held her tight and inhaled the smell of her hair. "Man Sarah, I'm so sorry about your sister. How is she doing? Is she awake?" He asked as he loosened his tight embrace so he could see her face.

Sarah stepped back, but didn't leave his arms. "She's still sleeping. She's getting stronger and the doctor is very pleased with her progress. Hopefully he will wake her soon. I am so glad you are here Mitch. I missed you."

Mitch smiled and stared at her. "You are beautiful, Sarah. So beautiful. You look exhausted though. And stressed, but so beautiful. Are you going to let me take you to dinner tonight?" He smiled, slipping his arm down to hold her hand and picking up his bag with his free hand.

"My father has ordered me to be absent tonight. I was told to go out with you and enjoy your company and stay away from the hospital and phone. Janelle is just in limbo, they feel confident about her stability, so an evening off will be ok. Dad insists. He thinks I need to be with someone who is here just for me. He thinks I need to debrief." Her smile was radiant.

"Well, let's see what we can do to enjoy the evening."

Sarah and Mitch took a cab back to the hotel. "I suppose I better get checked into my room and showered. I went to the airport straight from work. Maybe we can find a happy hour close by and decide where to go to dinner," Mitch said as they got out of the cab.

"Mitch, I have two beds in my room. You could just stay with me, the room is already paid for another week. Well, if you want. I don't mean to sound like I am being pushy or forward or, well. It's just a possibility, it is completely up to you." Sarah was fidgeting and acting nervous. She closed her eyes and began to shake her head for her silly behavior.

"Open your eyes, silly. I will stay in your room and I will be a gentleman, deal?" He was laughing, but not at her.

"I am rather embarrassed at this moment Mitch. I will recover my dignity while you take a shower." Sarah smiled at him, her cheeks blushed pink.

Mitch kissed her nose and said with a teasing growl, "Come on woman and take me to your room."

***

Mitch showered and dressed quickly. Sarah asked at the front desk and found that the there was a nice bar/restaurant within walking distance. Walk they did.

Sarah and Mitch sat at a highboy table in the corner. "Sarah, what do you want to drink?" asked Mitch as the waitress approached. "I would like a white wine, please," Sarah answered both to Mitch and the waitress at the same time.

"A Manhattan, please." Mitch smiled at the waitress.

The drinks arrived as Sarah and Mitch sat across from each other holding hands across the table.

"Your cat misses you, Sarah. He attacks me every morning promptly at 4:45 a.m. and won't leave me alone until I feed him." Mitch laughed as he spoke.

"Sorry you took him? I could have asked someone to come feed him. He is rather spoiled."

"No, not sorry. Just enlightened into your rather strange home life, sweet Sarah." Mitch scooted his chair over beside her, but faced her on the stool. "I want to kiss you, Sarah." And he did.

His kiss was soft, barely touching. Sarah felt his lips press slightly harder and his hand slide from her arm up under her hair. She started to relax into the kiss and responded to his warmth. He tipped her chin and ended the kiss. "Wow," he said quietly to her with his forehead pressed against hers. "You are like honey. I have missed you so much this week. I wanted to be here with you every moment, Sarah. I was so relieved when you called. I really thought I had done something wrong when you didn't answer the phone when I called you Monday and Tuesday."

"Oh Mitch, I was just so caught up in Janelle. I didn't mean to make you wonder. I am here now and so are you. For tonight you have my undivided attention. That is all I can promise for now. Once Janelle is better and can come home, then..."

He kissed her again. "Tonight is enough."

"Take me dancing Mitch. They have a dance floor at the bar. I want you to dance with me." She softly subtly pleaded.

"You say that now. When we are dancing you may regret the request. I cannot refuse you Sarah. Let's have dinner and then we can dance." Mitch rolled his eyes playfully. "If anyone can call what I do dancing."

They sat through a wonderful dinner and talked as they had while horseback riding. Mitch told her all about what had been happening at work and reassured her that no one minded her being gone. A slow song began to play. Sarah looked longingly at the band. She had asked once, she would let him make the offer now.

Mitch placed his hand backwards across his brow mocking a drama moment "It's time, Sarah. We can't put this off any longer. Dance with me." He feigned breathlessness and reached for her as he stood to take her to the dance floor.

Sarah melted against Mitch as he pulled her to him. He held her hand in his against his chest and his other arm rested in the small of her back. She smiled up at him as he moved her slowly around the floor. Mitch could dance and he knew it, teasing her could not be helped though.

"You are quite wonderful to hold Sarah." Mitch whispered against her hair as she placed her head against his chest.

"Oh Mitch. How is it possible that I feel I have belonged in your arms my whole life?"

"We were made for this moment Sarah. I can't explain it. It may be the emotion that is running so high right now, and I don't plan on taking advantage, but I know this isn't a temporary thing with you." He turned her slowly as they danced.

Sarah's entire being heated as he pressed against her. She wanted to feel alive. She had been so afraid and so hurting for Janelle. All she felt holding close to him was safe. Safe and home. Without realizing what was happening she began to feel tears run down her cheek. Mitch held her closer. Her tears turned to silent sobs. He held her even tighter and slowed their step. He wanted to allow her the freedom without causing a scene that would make her uncomfortable.

"Mitch," she sobbed into his chest, "please take me out of here."

***

They made their way back to the hotel room.

Sarah apologized for what she called her "melt down" all the way back. When they walked in, Mitch shut and locked the door behind them.

"I am going to run you a hot bath Sarah." He walked toward the bathroom.

"No Mitch, I'm sorry. I don't want to end the evening." She begged.

"It isn't ended Sarah. Once you are in the tub and covered in bubbles, I will bring you a glass of wine and we will talk some more. I want you to relax. A hot bath is the best remedy for surviving my so called dancing." He smiled.

Sarah laughed and grabbed her robe. She pulled her hair up into a clip and stood at the bathroom door. She wanted him to hold her. On the dance floor, in the tub. Just hold her. "Don't ruin this Sarah," she shouted silently in her own head.

Mitch stood and kissed her nose. He handed her a washcloth and stepped aside so she could come into the bathroom. They could both feel the heat from the hot tub filling the room. "Call me when it is safe to come in."

Sarah disrobed and then slinked into the hot tub and let the warmth flow over her. He was being wonderful to her she thought to herself. How stupid to burst into tears while dancing. He must think she is weak. Sarah was lost in thought. There was a quiet tap on the door.

"Sarah. Want your wine?" Mitch was talking quietly, afraid to disturb her thoughts or her rest.

"Come in Mitch," she said. "It's safe."

As Mitch opened the door and moved to sit on the foot stool by the bathtub he thought she was anything but safe. "You look quite relaxed there ma'am with bubbles framing your face and steam all around," he advised with a calm he was certainly not feeling.

Sarah sighed with her eyes closed. "This may be the nicest order I have ever followed, Mitch. Thank you for being so kind to me."

"I may just have ulterior motives Sarah. I may be trying to make you fall in love with me. What with my stellar dance moves, and filling you with white wine, I may succeed. Back washed?" He asked.

She sat up and just stared at him. She wanted to tell him that she was in love with him, but he would think her silly. "Back washed." Sarah handed him the washcloth.

Mitch rubbed her back with the cloth. She was beautiful. He loved the water dripping off her shoulders. He leaned down and kissed her shoulder. Sarah looked over toward him and tilted her head toward his mouth. She wanted to be kissed. Mitch knew it. Sarah knew it. Mitch obliged. He lowered his head and kissed her completely. Mitch curled his fingers in Sarah's hair. She turned toward him and slipped up to her knees. He slid his hand down her warm, soapy back until his hand rested on the curve of her hip. He knew this was happening way too fast. Sarah was very vulnerable and he would not push her emotions. Sarah wrapped her arms around him. Mitch took both of her arms in his hands and pulled his mouth from hers. He tipped his head back. He could not look at her naked breasts covered in soap suds in front of him. He knew that would push him over the edge. "Sarah. Sarah." Mitch whispered behind very controlled emotions. "You need to finish your bath. I promised to behave. If I feel your body next to me, or under my hands, I can't keep that promise." He looked at her face. Her eyes were dark and hungry. Her lips were swollen from the kiss. *Oh Sarah*, he thought to himself.

"Mitch." His name alone pleaded the overwhelming

hunger she was feeling.

Mitch grabbed a towel and wrapped it around her shoulders. "Sarah, I am going to walk out of here. I am going to go to bed and keep my promise to you. Finish your bath. Get dressed and talk to me from your bed, covered up, to your chin so I can't see any of your rosy red skin." He wanted to kiss her, but didn't dare.

Sarah's eyes welled with tears. She was so raw. She wanted him so much. "Don't go Mitch."

"Get dressed beautiful. Water was certainly made for your body, Sarah. Get dressed." He sounded curt. Sarah was not so naive as to realize that she had affected him. Mitch walked out of the bathroom.

Sarah tossed the towel onto the counter and sat back down in the water. The tears began to fall. She sobbed into the wash cloth, her tears flowed and she cried out of control. There were no thoughts accompanying the tears, just a body that wanted so much that it could not have.

Mitch got out of his clothes and into boxer shorts. He crawled into bed, turned down the light and listened to her muffled sobbing. All he wanted to do was go back in the bathroom and grab her out of the water. She needed to cry herself out. She needed to let it all out. Mitch was glad if he caused her wall to break. He wasn't enjoying what the kiss was doing for his body, but he was a man, not a boy, and he could handle not making love to her until it was right.

Sarah finally stopped crying. The water was cold. She pulled the drain plug with her toe and stood. She dried off and wrapped the towel around her. There was no steam left in the bathroom. Mitch must have fallen asleep she thought. *Wow, you are quite a beauty with your red eyes and nose Sarah. Could you be higher maintenance?* She asked her reflection in the mirror. Sarah brushed her teeth and opened the bathroom door. She could immediately smell his cologne. She was overcome with intense desire to be held and loved by Mitch. She stood in the door waiting for the moment to pass.

"Mitch?" She whispered. "Are you awake?"

"I am. Are you ok?" His voice was so gentle, questioning her without pressing.

Her tears slowly began again. She felt so helpless and alone. "Mitch." She stopped.

"Hmm?" He couldn't speak.

Sarah stood silently for a moment and then walked toward the bed. She sat down on her bed, towel wrapped tightly around her body, and looked at Mitch until her eyes adjusted to the light. When she could make out his face, his eyes were open and he was staring at her.

He smiled quickly with one side of his mouth and raised himself to one arm resting on his pillow.

"Mitch," she whispered even quieter and filled with emotion. The sound of her voice was tearing at him. He had to protect her. He had to make her world right again.

"Will you hold me, Mitch? Just for a little while. I just need to feel you hold me."

Mitch reached one arm to her and scooted to the middle of his bed. Sarah slid in the bed beside him and snuggled back into his body. The towel had risen up and Mitch could feel her behind pressed against his thighs. He sighed heavily and wrapped his arms tighter around hers to hold her. The two laid together quietly. Mitch's responses were on high alert. He thought that Sarah had fallen asleep. He wiggled his thighs away from her behind. His body was responding and he certainly did not want her to think he couldn't control himself. God she was a beautiful woman. He thought about how beautiful she looked covered in soap suds. He groaned silently as his body screamed at him for satisfaction.

Sarah felt him stir. She rolled in his arms and touched his face. He was tight jawed and wide awake. She bit his lower lip. "Sarah," he breathed afraid if he said more he would lose all control.

"I want you Mitch. I want you to make love to me. I want to feel you all over me." She kissed him and pushed her breasts against his chest.

He froze. Sarah misinterpreted this as rejection. She started to sit up and grabbed for the towel. "I am sorry Mitch." Her voice sounded so hurt.

Mitch caught her around the waist and pulled the towel away from her. "I just want you to be sure Sarah. I don't want to take advantage of your pain. I want you so badly that I can't think. If you want me, really want me, I will make love to you Sarah. Just ask me again."

Sarah leaned in slowly to kiss him. She spoke against his open mouth while kissing him. "I want you Mitch. I so want you."

That was all the encouragement Mitch needed. He rolled her underneath him and began kissing her face and her neck. The two of them loved gently, looking into each other's eyes as their desires were sated. Sarah smiled and sighed. She buried her face into his neck and fell asleep. She had a fleeting thought the world was perfect before she drifted off to sleep.

Mitch lay awake for hours feeling her weight in his arms. Her face looked rested and content. He knew that would change as soon as she woke up and the real world came back demanding her attention. He was hopeful that she would not regret giving in to their desires. This was not why he came to Phoenix. He hoped he didn't have to explain that to her.

CHAPTER NINETEEN

Janelle opened her eyes. At first she was overcome by fear and confusion. Then it all came back to her. The accident, the surgery, being in Arizona. She remembered that the doctor was going to place her in a drug induced coma. When was he going to do that? Maybe she was doing better than he had expected and it wasn't necessary. Her thoughts continued to run ramped. She wondered where her family was. She wished she could turn her head, or move her arms. If she could she would push the button and call the nurse. "Hello," Janelle called to anyone who may be listening.

It must have worked because just as she finished the word a nurse walked in smiling from ear to ear. "Well, good morning Ms. Beckett. It is so wonderful to finally see you awake!" She was beaming at Janelle.

"Wow, how long did I sleep? It feels like only minutes," Janelle rasped at her. "I think I am thirsty, my throat is kind of dry and sore."

"Let me get your doctor and some water. I will also call your family. They have been waiting so patiently to see you." The nurse squeezed Janelle's hand and turned to walk out of the room.

Shortly thereafter Dr. Curtis walked in. "Welcome back Janelle. How do you feel?" he queried.

"I feel ok. I don't seem to hurt anywhere. Why did the nurse seem so surprised I was awake? I thought you felt good about the surgery. What about this coma thing? Did you decide you didn't have to do it?" Janelle was questioning nervously. She felt very emotional and could not explain why.

"Slow down, Janelle. Today is Tuesday. It has been two weeks since your surgery. You have been resting and asleep. It has done wonders for you. Physically I am very happy with your progress. Let's get you out of bed here soon." Dr. Curtis left to see whether the nurse had reached her family and to make arrangements for removing her catheter.

***

The phone rang in the hotel room. Sarah started awake and was momentarily confused at the feel of Mitch's body next to hers. As she started to relax back into him the phone rang again. She groaned sleepily and then the reality of the phone ringing hit her. She flew out of bed and grabbed the phone. She listened and made affirmative responses.

"We will be there immediately," Sarah stated to whomever had called her. She hung up the phone and turned to Mitch. She smiled at him. "Janelle is awake. She is awake. We can see her, Mitch!" Sarah ran to her suitcase and grabbed clothes to get dressed.

Mitch was thrilled at the news and got up to get dressed. Anything that needed to be said between them would have to wait. Janelle was awake. Everything else paled in comparison.

CHAPTER TWENTY

Kelly and Jake decided to fly back to Michigan to visit Kelly's sister. She needed to get away for a while. Her father in law's passing made her long to fix things with her mother and made her miss her family. Logan told her to go. He would see her in a few weeks.

Logan went to Phoenix. He had to be with Janelle. She was what made sense right now, and even if she didn't know it, she needed him there.

***

Logan walked into Janelle's hospital room. She was awake. "Hello," he exclaimed so completely thrilled to see her. "You're awake. I am so happy to see your beautiful eyes, Janelle."

"Hi," she said tentatively. She was so frustrated that she could not remember his name or his face. *God, please give me a hint who he is*, she thought to herself.

Logan talked with her about how strong she was and how he knew that her recovery would break the doctor's time table. She liked him. He was strong, strong for her. They had been visiting for about an hour when the nurse came in and told Janelle her sister and parents were on their way over from the hotel. Logan knew he would have to go.

"Janelle, I'll come back and see you in a day or so. I should go anyway. I just knew I wanted to see you. And to find you awake, wow. Now I know why I couldn't shake the need to get down here." He touched her cheek with his bent index finger and smiled. "You're as beautiful as ever!" He winked at her and then turned and left.

CHAPTER TWENTY-ONE

Janelle was in the hospital another week. She had little memory of the first two weeks, but the last one drug on. Plans were made for her to go to a Rehab House close by so she could be monitored by Dr. Curtis. The Becketts wanted her to come home to Texas. It wasn't possible. She would have to stay for two or three more weeks in the Rehab and then she would be able to leave. Janelle knew she had to figure out just what to do and where to go. Most likely to Sarah's.

***

Now that she was in rehab they allowed visitors almost any time she wanted them and she wasn't relearning how to walk. The break in her leg had been a bad one and it was expected that she would retain a slight limp. The back of her neck was still numb and the doctor told her it would get better, but would probably not completely subside. It had been almost five weeks since her surgery. She was supposed to get to go home soon. The only thing that made it worth it was that she was feeling better and her visits were longer.

Her parents had to leave to go home for various doctor's appointments and vowed to be back at the weekend. Her sister had to return to work and Janelle told her to go. She was very busy during the days and was enjoying Logan's company when he came to see her.

Logan came to see Janelle every other day. Janelle still wasn't one hundred percent sure why she knew him, but the pieces were coming together. He had told her about Shannon's Luck and seeing her there eating. She knew she had seen him there, but wasn't sure why he was still around. She hoped she hadn't missed or forgotten anything intimate that might have occurred between them. Her thoughts began to wander to how great he looked in tight jeans and how she knew he had rock hard thighs and abs. No, she certainly did not want to forget any encounters with that man. He was like no one she had ever seen.

"Wow," she mumbled to herself as she sat staring out the window at the Bird of Paradise plant. "Out of the hospital for eight days and already thinking about sex." She giggled. Janelle was in a great mood. She was feeling better and knew that Logan would be there for an early, long, lunch. She walked to the mirror with the help of her walker and looked at herself. She was able to kind of comb her hair, but could really do little else. The halo brace made hairdo's a tough one. "This is as good as you get for now, Jani. Accept it," she told herself tersely and turned toward the door. Logan was standing there with a guilty grin on his face.

"How long have you been standing there?" She asked blushing as she knew she had talked about sex out loud.

Logan's smile broadened, as if that were possible, and he titled his head, crossed his arms and leaned against the door jam. "Well...," he drawled slowly, "I seem to recall hearing something about how much better you are feeling and your need for extracurricular activity."

Goodness, it wasn't possible for a man to be that attractive she thought. Janelle felt herself blush more. She decided she needed to sit. "I need to sit, Logan," she whispered.

He reached for her elbow to help her and they both jumped. They both felt it. Electric and magic through an innocent touch.

After Janelle was seated she decided to come clean with him. He obviously cared about her and she knew it wasn't fair to deceive him about what she did and didn't remember.

"Logan, can you sit a minute before you go pick up lunch? I need to talk to you." Janelle looked down nervously at the chair she wanted him to sit in.

Logan sat down and thought to himself this is where Janelle would tell him she's married, engaged, or in a serious relationship with someone in Texas and that his visits need to stop. Janelle was talking, but with his mind wandering Logan had heard nothing.

"Janelle, wait, start over." Logan reached for her hand, forcing his mind to stop wandering so he could listen to what she was saying.

"I was saying that I have enjoyed you coming to see me lately. I feel like you are so comfortable with me, and I with you. It seems like there has been something here, you know, something longer than this past couple of weeks. I, I, oh Logan...," Janelle paused and a tear started to fall down her cheek.

"Jani," he cooed "Don't say anything that upsets you. Whatever it is, it's okay and it'll keep. I don't want you upset. Shhh, don't talk, it's okay."

"I have to Logan. I have to. It's just, well, I need to be honest with you about something, but I don't want to hurt you." Janelle paused, took a deep breath and closed her eyes.

Logan nodded and waited with a sinking feeling in the pit of his stomach.

"See, I don't remember the accident. At all. I don't remember actually even being in Flagstaff. I know that you are familiar to me, but Logan, I don't know why. I can't remember why I know you. It scares me because I remember everyone else I am supposed to remember." She stopped talking and looked at him. Not that she had a choice. If she wasn't wearing the halo brace she would turn her head away, or drop her head into her hands, or she would throw herself into his arms for comfort.

"Oh, Janelle, you only met me the day you had your accident. I met you at Shannon's Luck only about an hour before the accident. You stopped at the restaurant and had some lunch. We flirted a little. Well, I flirted a little with you. You responded, a little. I knew where you were going to stay, at the Mendoza's cabin. Do you remember you were going there?"

Janelle nodded, she did remember the vacation.

"Well, I decided to make sure you found the road you had to turn on since it is rather confusing."

Logan kneeled down in front of Janelle. He reached up and placed his hands gently on each of her cheeks. "You aren't supposed to remember me. I am sorry, I should have been clearer. My being around, while you were in the hospital and all, probably added to the confusion since only your sister and parents were there."

"Wow, Logan. How can I feel like you belong in my life

when I haven't even had a life since we met? Why did you come to Phoenix, why do you keep coming? You don't owe me, you know." Janelle was afraid now. She had interpreted his being there and coming to see her as a relationship and he was actually a stranger. This was all for pity or guilt. Janelle closed her eyes, again wishing she could hide her face by burying it in her hands.

"Janelle, listen to me." The softness in Logan's voice had waned slightly and his voice was confident in what he was saying. He needed her to understand what he could not even begin to explain to her. "Look at me, Janelle."

Janelle opened her eyes and her lips were pulled into a terse line. She was good at tucking her emotions behind logic. She was retreating there even as he spoke.

"Janelle, I was drawn to your determination and your pensiveness from the moment I saw you at Dad's place. Hiding there now, won't make me stop talking. Don't be mad. Just listen. I know you are thinking I am here because I feel somehow responsible, or out of pity. You are wrong, Janelle, wrong. You hear me?"

She wouldn't open her eyes to make eye contact with him. Why did this hurt so badly? Maybe the turmoil of her health was making her ultra-sensitive. She kept listening without response.

"When you were in that car wreck. When I saw you in that car. I thought you were dead. I was so scared. I begged you to hold on and tried to will you to survive. For some reason the paramedic must have thought we were family. They gave me information and let me see you when you were in the Flagstaff Emergency Room. I didn't want you to die alone. I knew you would make it if someone believed in you. So, I decided that since you had maneuvered your way into my heart at first glance, I was staying until you either, woke up and told me to get the hell away from you, or your family came and did it for you." He was speaking loudly now.

Janelle opened her tear-filled eyes. His words were so heartfelt and honest. "Logan," she started.

"No, Janelle. You need to listen," he continued speaking. "You were transferred down here to Phoenix and I drove down there so you wouldn't be alone. Same reason, plus since everyone thought I was with you, I felt like I was responsible for information until it could be given to your family. I knew someone had to be sure to reach your sister. You had already mentioned her to me at Dad's place and how she didn't really want you to come to Arizona in the first place." He stopped talking rather abruptly and silence sat between them for a few moments.

"Janelle, when they told me you might not survive the surgery, I realized something that made no sense then and probably makes little now. I realized I had always loved you. Somehow you finally made it into my life so I could continue loving you and I wasn't letting you go that easily. Do you remember the scare the doctor told you about when you were first coming around and all your vitals crashed?"

Janelle glanced up at him as he spoke and then dropped her eyes back down to her hands.

"I was there. It scared me. I told you that my Dad would have thought you to be a 'feisty little lass' and begged you to hold on. I told you I would be there and not let anyone take you away."

A memory flooded Janelle's mind. Her eyes snapped up to Logan as he spoke and her hand flew to her mouth. "Oh Logan. It was you. It was you who saved me when something I could not see held me down and was trying to drag me to darkness. It was you standing there. It was you who called me feisty little lass. Of course, that is why I see your face in my dreams. It was you." She was smiling and looked so relieved. He smiled too. Again, tears welled up in her eyes.

"You saved me, Logan. You saved me. She reached for his hands. "You love me?" Janelle smiled and her voice teased with a sing-song tone.

"Yep and not a damned thing I can do about it. Care to explain how I saved you?"

Janelle explained her dream. Logan explained that his father's name was Shannon. Shannon Logan. That he was Shannon Logan also, but everyone always called him Logan. The restaurant was his family's place. It was always Dad's place. He then went on to explain how his father had died this past two weeks and how she was one of few bright spots in his life. They talked for well over an hour and Logan had managed to place his arm around her, despite the halo brace. Janelle told him how much she had been looking forward to sitting on the porch of the A-Frame and watching all the birds in the trees, especially the beautiful blue birds. He made a note of her saying that, he would make it up to her somehow. She was euphoric with him sitting there and with his gentle affection.

"Logan, I am famished. Can we go eat now?" She smiled and the two walked down the hall to the cafeteria and continued talking over lunch until it was time for him to go. "I will be back Thursday ok? I might even see if I can free you from this place." He placed a kiss on her cheek and was gone.

CHAPTER TWENTY-TWO

Thursday came and Logan came to visit too. He stood at the door and asked her to close her eyes. When she did he placed a wrapped package on her lap. Janelle smiled like a small child. She was excited to see him again and very excited he brought her a gift.

"Oh Logan, you didn't have to bring me a present." Janelle was beaming at him as she reached to open the package.

"Oh well, it isn't really a present, more of a small sample of what I promise to make up to you later." Logan smiled at her.

"Hmmm," she said in his direction in a teasing tone. "Can I open this in public, will I blush?"

"You can open it, go on. What could you possibly be implying?" He spoke with a mock scolding tone to his voice.

Janelle opened the package to reveal a delicate brass painted wrought iron cage. In it was a small blue velvet and feathered imitation bluebird. It was beautiful and perched on a small swing. Its tail, made of feathers, extended almost to the bottom of the cage. She instantly knew that this was because of their conversation about the blue birds and the porch.

"Oh Logan. I just love it." she exclaimed and reached awkwardly to hug him. "I am sorry, this brace just gets in the way. Consider yourself hugged properly though."

"Well, when you are allowed out of here, I will take you out to a great place I know where there are trees everywhere, deciduous trees and birds flying all around. You will love it. Deal?" He arched an eyebrow at her and smiled.

"Deal, Logan. I think I am going to be going home to Texas in a week or so. Maybe before then. I really want to figure out what to do about school. I hate that I am, once again, not able to go. It's almost as if I am not supposed to go to law school. Every time I start, or have a plan in place, something happens. I am going to finish my Bachelor's Degree, I have to do that." She was talking out loud to Logan, but Janelle was miles away.

"I finished my degree at Northern Arizona University. I finished it in Business with a minor in

Sociology. You might consider it. You could stay locally and then when you felt more up to it, you could take your classes at ASU Law School. I would be very willing to help you with your driving. Well, it's an option. I know you probably really want to get back to Texas." Logan didn't want his disappointment at her leaving to come through in his voice. She had a lot to do with just recovering, he didn't want to press her.

"Actually Logan, I don't want to go back to Texas at all. I had planned on being here at least three years. So, I am sort of having to start over. I have to still make decisions on what happens after the doctor takes this damned brace off and lets me get on with my life. I am hopeful that I can stop using this cane or walker real soon too. I guess I have to get better physically and that means I'll have to go back to Texas because I can't go back to work yet and really can't stay by myself. Sarah said I can come stay with her. So, since I will have lost all my A-Frame time being in the hospital and being here, I guess I am going back to Texas." She was disappointed, but reminded herself silently that she could be dead.

"What if I could get you that A-Frame, Janelle? Would you want to stay?" He posed the question to her more as a matter of fact statement.

"How would you manage that? It was paid for two full months, which, as you know are almost over!"

"I know Mr. Mendoza. Carlos and his wife are incredible people. He is aware of what happened to you and actually offered Scott his money back. I know he isn't someone who insists the cabin is rented all the time. What if I talk to him and ask him to transfer your time from this past two months, to the next two months? By then you should be able to rent a place of your own and we can figure out what to do then." Logan just didn't want her to leave Arizona.

"Wow, Logan. I am sort of overwhelmed. I never considered that a possibility. My sister and parents would probably freak out. I will think about it, okay? I will." She was probably more afraid that if she wanted to stay Mr. Mendoza would say "no" than afraid of what her family would think.

"I am going to just check in to it, okay. I won't make a commitment, I will just see what Carlos and Lupita have planned for the place for the next few months," he told her.

The rest of the afternoon was incredible. Logan told her he had things this coming weekend that had to be taken care of. He hated that he would not be able to come to see her until Monday, but promised he would be early and that he would call her Saturday.

Janelle was disappointed that she wouldn't get to see him, but her sister would be here this weekend and she was glad they would have the time together without anyone else there. They had some long catching up to do.

CHAPTER TWENTY-THREE

Saturday. Sarah arrived at 10:30 a.m. She hugged Janelle as best she could. "God you look great, Janelle. Your cheeks have all the color back. Wow, this place is sure agreeing with you. I am just kidding. I can't wait to get you home!"

"Oh, Sarah. I am so glad you are here. We have so much catching up to do." Janelle could not let go of her sister's hand.

The sisters sat and talked and giggled as if they were teenagers. Sarah told Janelle about Mitch and how incredible things were going.

"I have a confession, Jani," Sarah whispered. "I slept with him." She stopped talking and made a mock stunned face at Janelle.

"What? Oh my goodness, Sarah," Janelle laughed. "Well, is he incredible?"

Sarah laughed, "Oh yes. And....well, he already asked me to marry him." She looked up at Janelle.

"Now you must be kidding. Sarah you don't even know him!" Janelle scolded.

"I can't explain it. I feel I have always known him. This is right, Janelle. I haven't answered him. I told him everything was happening too fast. He agreed we would talk again in a couple of weeks, or months. He just wanted me to know he wants to marry me." She beamed at Janelle.

"Wow, you love him. I can see it. Take your time and be sure, but if you love him go for it. We both know that tomorrow isn't promised to us. If you want to grab the brass ring today, grab it." Janelle was leading up to something and Sarah knew it.

"Spill it Janelle. I can see a scheme brewing in your brain. What are you planning to do that you know Mom and Dad won't approve of?" Sarah was laughing, but serious. Janelle was always brave and no one ever knew what she was going to decide to do next.

"Well, what would you say if...," she hesitated and stared at her sister. Her smile continued to grow until she was almost giggling. "You won't believe this."

"Spill it. I can't wait to hear what it is that you have to say." She knew she wasn't going to like it given Janelle's current medical condition.

"Logan thinks he can get Mr. Mendoza, the man who owns the A-Frame I reserved, to let me rent it for two months from when I get out of here. I am thinking about doing it and then I can take some of my classes at the University in Flagstaff. There. What do you think?" She looked at Sarah as if she expected a hug and well wishes.

"Are you absolutely insane? Janelle. Please. Seriously, what do you really even know about this guy?" Sarah was just plain irritated at this announcement as if Janelle had decided to buy cowboy boots or something. Not to mention that Sarah wasn't so all fired sure that Logan wasn't already married, or involved with the blonde he saw. Did he even bother to tell Jani that he had a child? Sarah seriously doubted it. Sarah closed her eyes, took a deep breath, put her hands out at her side and pressed them down into the air. It was a gesture that said "Okay, enough. Regroup."

"Janelle," Sarah started. "Ok, let's say for a minute that this is a sane idea you are having. Do you really think that a total stranger is going to want to be there every time you need something? Do you really think that you can trust him to be there every time you can't reach something or need help up? What if you have some kind of relapse? What happens in two months when you have to leave the cabin? Have you thought about any of this?" Sarah sounded irritated. "I know I am probably a little protective of you right now, I mean having almost lost you and all in that damned car wreck, but even if you hadn't had to reattach your head, I would be wondering what the hell you were thinking, Janelle!" Sarah's voice had escalated as she spoke.

"Sarah. Lower your voice and please stop talking to me as if I am five. I had intended all along to come here for two months and then move to an apartment by ASU, right? This plan isn't too far from the original one. I just need a little help, that's all. You come in here and announce to me that you slept with a man that you have only known since my accident and that you are planning on getting married and you are asking me if I am sane. Come on, Sarah! Don't set a different standard for me than you set for yourself." Janelle felt stronger just bantering with her sister over this issue. The argument itself was helping her make up her mind and she decided to let Sarah know that very fact.

"You know Sarah, this started out as a "what if"

scenario. This discussion with you has just about convinced me that it is a perfect idea." Janelle then sat quiet.

"I didn't come here to fight with you Janelle. I just don't think this is a great idea on your part. By the way, I have known Mitch for over two years. We only dated the first week you left. Don't forget that, Janelle. I am going to get a soda. When I come back we can regroup and we won't talk about this. You have a couple weeks still before you have to make the decision, right? Let's see how you feel then." Janelle nodded and Sarah stood to go get her soda.

Just as she stood, the room became instantly hot, her head started spinning and she almost passed out. Sarah grabbed for the seat and fell in her chair. She took a couple of deep breaths and the dizziness passed.

Janelle moved towards her. "Damn Sarah are you ok? What happened? Want me to call someone? Janelle was stroking Sarah's hair gently and having a moment of guilt thinking the argument they were having upset her more than she realized.

"I'm fine. I'm fine. I don't know why that happened. I might be hungry. I didn't eat breakfast and had a real early dinner. Want to go get something to eat? I am feeling better now." Sarah started to stand.

"Sarah, just sit for a few minutes. I can go get us something to eat, or we can go when you aren't dizzy." Janelle wasn't letting her fall. She had never seen her sister pass out, or even near pass out.

"I'm fine now, really. It's just as if that never happened. I feel fine again. Let's go eat." Sarah stood again and there was no dizziness. The sisters left the room and went to the cafeteria.

Sarah made a mental note, this was her third dizzy

spells in two days. She didn't think anything was really wrong, but if it continued she was going to the doctor. Maybe her blood pressure was messed up she thought to herself.

CHAPTER TWENTY-FOUR

The next week went by as had the weeks before it. Dr. Curtis came to see Janelle on Friday late afternoon after Logan had left. Janelle was still deciding what to do. Logan had assured her that Carlos Mendoza was willing to let her take her two months now. Sarah and her parents were insistent that she come home. She had to decide by next week, she had to make plans. She expected to go home by next weekend.

"Hello Janelle," Dr. Curtis announced as he walked in her room. He was all business.

"Hi there Doc. When are you going to get me out of here? I really want to leave," Janelle announced.

"Well, that is part of what I am here for. Your last x-ray and MRI series show that your bones have fused nicely. The graft is working exactly as we had hoped. I plan to remove your halo brace Friday, Janelle. You can go home this weekend. I will fit you for a hard neck brace to wear for a month or so. Your neck muscles have atrophied to some degree and I don't think you will be able to completely hold your head straight enough at this point.

I also want some more time to pass before you have free range of motion." Dr. Curtis knew she would be pleased at the news. She had recovered nicely and other than some residual numbness at the incision sight, she was doing well. The team decided she would heal better at home and out of this medical environment. She was out of danger and was a walking miracle.

"Oh Dr. Curtis, I could kiss you." Janelle stood and gave him the mock hug she had perfected in her halo brace. Tears of happiness were streaming down her face. "This is a phone call I cannot wait to make. Maybe I will wait and just surprise my sister when she comes out this weekend."

"Well, you probably need to make plans Janelle. Plans to get back to Texas. You also may want her here when we remove the brace. It is a little scary. The moral support will be great and to be honest with you, it is going to be rather painful." Dr. Curtis always hated the pain involved in removing the screws from the skull.

"Oh no," Janelle said sounding slightly downtrodden by that news. "I hadn't thought about it hurting to remove this thing. I guess I was asleep through most of the painful stage and have been fortunate that the screws haven't pulled out or anything. Ok, I will call Sarah tonight."

"It is only temporary pain, Janelle. Nothing compared to what you have been through. I have enjoyed caring for you. You have a great strength about you. Without it, I would not have performed this operation. You still need to be careful you know. I will get a good referral in Abilene for you to report in for ongoing care, okay?" The doctor stood.

"Dr. Curtis. I can't thank you enough. If you had not

been willing to take that surgical chance, I would have died. That is a very overwhelming thought I so appreciate your belief in trying something new." Janelle touched his shoulder, it was intended to express all the gratitude she was feeling.

"Your ability to stand here and talk to me instead of the alternative is all the thanks I need. It is also what makes me believe in this surgery. In time I am hopeful more Surgeons will learn and agree with it. Too many head injury victims die with no chance for recovery. You get well and live your life to the fullest Janelle. That is thanks enough. Well, I have to go make rounds. I will see you Friday." Dr. Curtis smiled at Janelle and winked before he walked out of the room.

For a few minutes Janelle just sat and smiled. She was so happy. Then she called Sarah and her parents. Her father was extremely ill and unable to travel to Arizona and her mother would not leave him. Sarah intended to be there Friday at noon. The brace would come off after the doctor conducted his afternoon rounds. She was going to call Logan, but the more she thought the better plan she was able to pull together. Janelle decided that she would have Sarah drive her to Flagstaff over the weekend before the flight to Texas. Janelle would casually mention to Logan she was considering staying and see how serious he was about her staying. If his reaction confirmed what she already believed, that is, that he wanted her to stay and was going to be there for her, then she would stay in Flagstaff. Then Sarah would return to Phoenix, and then to Texas, without her. If Logan acted put out or as if his offer had been out of guilt or pity, she would simply tell him her mind was not made up and then she would just plan to go home No hard feelings. She hoped he wanted her to stay.

CHAPTER TWENTY-FIVE

Friday finally came. Logan was there early just as he had been for weeks. Janelle was positively giddy at the thought of losing the brace and of getting out of there. Logan thought she had one more week. He laughed at her several times during the visit and knew that she had cabin fever.

"Janelle, you are certainly feeling the effects of being stuck here for so long. I bet you can't wait to get out next week, can you?" He smiled as he spoke.

"I am just happy to be alive, Logan. I want so much to just get on with my life. My family is elated I will be out of here. It is certainly time." She didn't dare broach the subject of staying. He hadn't said much more about it since he told her that Mr. Mendoza was agreeable to her staying. She had checked in to classes at NAU just in case she decided to stay. Sarah had told her that insurance had replaced her car. Perhaps if she stayed Sarah would bring it here and fly back. Time would tell. She would tell Sarah this evening, after the brace was off, about her final decision.

***

Sarah woke on Friday and her first thought was that she was going to get her sister. The brace was coming off and Janelle could come home and start her life over. The second thought was that she felt awful. The thought of even rolling over to get up made her stomach lurch. What in the world is wrong she wondered? It felt like a flu she just couldn't come down with. If she didn't feel better, significantly better, by Monday when they got home, she was going to call her doctor. The dizziness had not stopped and now this flu. She must be run down from the stress. Sarah looked over at Mitch sleeping peacefully beside her. He had held her so sweetly last night. The two had never talked about the night they spent together in Phoenix, but moved comfortably into a cherished relationship. Sarah hated leaving him for the weekend since it was usually the only time they had for more than dinner or a phone call.

Monday would be here soon enough and she would not have to leave him again on the weekends. She had thought long and hard about the marriage issue. Her heart told her that marrying Mitch was the right thing to do. Her logical mind, not that she used it much around him, tried to reason her out of it. "Logic," she mumbled and rolled closer to Mitch. He instinctively reached for her, but never woke. Sarah lay in his arms perfectly content until a wave of nausea made her jump out of bed and sent her running for the bathroom. Great. Sarah had to fly in five hours and couldn't even stand. She started to worry that she would give Janelle her flu. This was not good. Janelle probably couldn't handle throwing up if she got sick. What would that do for her fusing bones? Sarah wanted to ask Mitch to retrieve Sarah, but knew that she had to be there. Sarah went back to bed and when she woke Mitch had already gotten up and was down the hall watching the news and drinking coffee.

"Hey, you feeling alright, Sarah?" He asked knowing Sarah wasn't one to stay in bed.

"I had a rough time earlier this morning. Now I am feeling better, great actually. Maybe I should eat. Almost time to go get my sister. I can't wait for her to be here. Do you think it will be weird with her here, Mitch? I mean, are you going to be ok with still coming over? I could come to your place and all." Sarah questioned him.

"Sarah, Janelle will always be part of my life as long as she stays part of yours. If you and she are okay with me being here from time to time, what needs to change?" He moved in and held her face as he placed a kiss on her nose. "Get dressed. You are not going to Phoenix in that outfit!!"

CHAPTER TWENTY-SIX

Dr. Curtis came in to the exam room. Sarah had driven Janelle there. The people at the rehab were incredible to her when she left. Everyone wished her well. Everyone told her to heal and live happy. She certainly intended to.

Dr. Curtis had given Janelle something to make her relax. He injected some anesthetic into the areas around the screws. One by one he removed them. Janelle cried despite the pain treatment. The last screw was removed and her head was wrapped. She was fitted with a plastic neck brace that dipped down in the front and back and was so high that she still could not move her head. After this was over, Janelle fell asleep on the exam table. Dr. Curtis expected this and left Sarah to sit with her until she woke.

Janelle was released from Dr. Curtis' care and told to check in with a spine injury specialist he had referred her to in Abilene. She was expected to have weekly appointments until it was determined she could move to a soft brace and eventually remove the brace all together.

Sarah and Janelle went to Sarah's hotel room. Janelle

was so thrilled to be out in public. They stopped at the local coffee house and enjoyed a latte before heading to bed.

"Sarah. I have an idea. I know you don't want to entertain this thought, but I really want to stay in Arizona. I just don't want to retreat to Texas. I have to move forward. I want to drive to Flagstaff tomorrow and just see Logan. I will be able to tell if he really wants me to stay in town or if it was a pity invite. If he wants me to stay Sarah, I am going to. If he seems he doesn't want to, then I will go home with you Sunday. Will you drive me to Flagstaff tomorrow?" Janelle looked resolved and hopeful.

Sarah knew that she would only make matters worse if she fought her. "Janelle, I'll drive you, but I need to ask you something. Has Logan ever mentioned a wife, or girlfriend and a child?" She asked her cautiously. Maybe there was an explanation.

"What? No! Logan isn't married. Why would you even ask me that?" She stammered at her.

"Well, when you were in the ICU I saw him at the hospital as he was leaving. You were still asleep and I saw him at a distance."

Sarah started to tell her the rest. All about the tall blonde woman who took his arm and the little boy, two maybe three years old that he carried in his arms. She could not bring herself to say it. "Janelle, did Logan ever...?" She began to put the question a different way. Just as she started Janelle interrupted.

"No. Sarah. Logan never. Just stop. I don't even want to hear what you are going to say. I know Logan meant what he said to me. I know he isn't a murderer, a thief, a crazy man, married, or anything else you want to accuse him of. So stop. Just stop. Sarah you are upsetting me for no reason. Just please stop. Will you just drive me to Flagstaff? Please." Clearly Janelle was frustrated and angry. Was it out of fear that Sarah may have a point, that she didn't really know Logan? She didn't care. She was following her heart on this one. "Sarah, sometimes we have to let our so completely in control and planned out lives get a little messy. I want to do this. Please. Please just drive me to Flagstaff and be happy for me."

The tone in Janelle's voice told Sarah the discussion was over. She didn't want to fight with her sister. She loved Janelle and wanted only to protect her, but it wasn't her life to live. Sarah knew she needed to let this play out and just be there if her sister needed her.

"I will, I will. Let's just finish our coffee and go back to the hotel. Flagstaff is a long drive." The sisters sat and finished their coffee. Afterward they headed back to the hotel and watched a movie before going to sleep.

CHAPTER TWENTY-SEVEN

Morning came and Sarah helped Janelle get ready. The hard neck brace created different challenges for Janelle. She was happy about being able to shower and to fix her hair since it had been just combed and pulled into a ponytail for so long. Janelle wanted to make special effort today. She wore an outfit Sarah had brought for her. Green denim jeans and a corset like top. Without the brace Janelle would have thought herself looking rather attractive. With the brace, she felt bulky.

"Wow, Janelle. He is going to want you to stay there just to have your beautiful face and body to look at once or twice a week. I know you are nervous. Don't be. Remember what you told me. If this is meant to be, then it will happen." Sarah tried her best to be supportive. She smiled as she spoke. Just for Janelle. No, Sarah did not want her sister to stay in Arizona, but then she had not wanted her to come here in the first place, even before the accident. This was about Janelle. It was not about her and Sarah accepted that fact.

"Thank you, Sarah. Thank you for not fighting me on

this and for driving me to Flagstaff. Somehow I feel that the beginning of my life is about to happen. Not my career, or even my schooling, but my life. This just feels like the path I am supposed to take. Sarah. I know you understand. I am very grateful that you are here with me. Of course, if this turns out badly...," Janelle let her voice drift into silence. She really didn't want to entertain what she would do if Logan hadn't actually meant the things he said to her.

"Let's go, Sis. It'll work out fine." Sarah picked up her sweater, water bottle and purse. Janelle followed.

Sarah and Janelle were enjoying the ride toward Flagstaff. They sang all the songs on the radio, well at least the ones where they knew the words. They looked off at mountains in the distance and admired and commented on how the terrain changed every few hundred feet. They were both hungry and decided it was time to stop and eat. Sarah pulled off the highway and found a restaurant.

"It is sure going to feel good to stretch my legs," Janelle commented. She got out of the rental car and did just that. Janelle turned to smile at Sarah just as Sarah fell toward the car door.

"Sarah! Oh no, are you okay?" Janelle moved quickly to Sarah's side of the car.

"I'm fine, I'm fine. I just can't seem to spend the morning being hungry anymore. I get dizzy if I don't eat," Sarah said nervously laughing and trying to make light of it for Janelle's sake. Truth was, it was starting to scare Sarah.

"You are scaring me. This has happened three times in front of me, Sarah. Has it happened more often than that?" Janelle pressed Sarah. Something was not right and she did not want to have her sister ignore something so serious.

"It's happened a time or two more. But always in the morning when I wait to eat. I will see a doctor when I get home. Maybe it's my blood pressure or something." Sarah was trying not to sound worried.

After Sarah's dizziness passed the two went into the restaurant to have something to eat. Sarah assured Janelle she would feel better after she got food in her stomach. Janelle ordered a western omelet with hash browns, English muffin and coffee. Sarah ordered her eggs scrambled with a side of fruit, toast and coffee.

"Oh man, Sarah. I haven't had a decent meal since Shannon's Luck. This is so good," Janelle announced with all the emphasis she could muster on 'so good!' "I could eat a whole 'nother plate of this food." Manners were temporarily out the window as Janelle spoke while chewing her food.

"You have been very deprived of good food lately. Hospital food, despite their best efforts, is always hospital food. It is the stuff that jokes are made of you know." Sarah was smiling at Janelle eating. Sarah was glad Janelle's nerves seemed to have settled about the trip and even more pleased Janelle wasn't pushing about the dizzy spells Sarah kept having.

They finished their meals, paid the bill and headed to the car so they could get back on the road. It was about another hour to Flagstaff and then thirty or so minutes through to the turn off for Shannon's Luck. Janelle was excited and in a hurry to get to Shannon's Luck.

Janelle could not wait for Sarah to see Shannon's Luck. From there Janelle would call Logan and let him know she was in Flagstaff for the day. She hoped he would be so surprised that she was out of the inpatient rehab a week early that he would either invite her to come to his place or drive over to meet them at Shannon's Luck for lunch. She knew Logan would be happy her halo brace was off. Her hair covered the small bandages on her forehead the best Janelle could make it, but she still knew Logan would be happy to see her partial freedom.

Finally they arrived. It was an uncomfortable trip for Janelle. Her first day out of her halo brace was proving what Dr. Curtis had said. Her neck muscles were atrophied. Her neck was very sore and she had developed a pretty significant headache.

Janelle sat with her eyes closed as Sarah stopped the car. "Janelle," Sarah said softly. "Are you sleeping?"

"No, Sarah. I am just having a tough time adjusting to any type of self-support for my neck. Do you have any pain reliever?"

"Yes." She reached in her purse and handed

Janelle some pain reliever. Janelle took the pills and then closed her eyes again.

"Sarah can we just sit a few minutes before we go inside?" Janelle asked her sister.

"Certainly. The view here is very pretty. We can enjoy this and give those pills a chance to kick in."

"Thank you. I do need to let it kick in. Dr. Curtis gave me a prescription for something stronger that I really hoped I wouldn't need. I should have taken it," she said quietly to Sarah as she rested her eyes waiting for the pain to subside. "I'm going to sit here awhile. Look around and tell me what you see. It will be like a trip through my 'happy place' and maybe I can relax more."

Sarah began to describe the different colors of greens

that were seen in the Evergreens, the Sycamore, the Fir trees and the tall weeds growing. She described the little yellow flower bushes. The flowers looked like miniature Sunflowers. Sarah loved them. Sarah also saw a Cardinal and a Blue Jay, both of which she described to Janelle in great detail and with an excitement in her voice that expressed even more about their beauty than her words ever could.

"I get it, Janelle. I get how you knew you would love it here and how the vacation time here would be so perfect after the hectic year you have just gone through," Sarah spoke sincerely as she admired the world around her.

Janelle smiled and opened her eyes. She turned, as best she could, towards Sarah. "I never had the chance to sit and enjoy it. I want to do that now though. I feel better. Want to go in?"

Sarah and Janelle entered Shannon's Luck. Janelle led, walking toward the small bar and hoped Frank would be working. He was.

***

"As I live and breathe," Frank gave a hearty laugh as he spoke. "Logan told me about your recovery, but he didn't tell me you were out of the hospital, Janelle."

"Hi there, Frank. I guess everyone here would've heard about the accident. I hear it was really awful. I find myself quite lucky to have survived not only the accident, but my surgery and recovery. Logan doesn't actually know I'm out. I wanted it to be a surprise." Janelle perched herself on the barstool and smiled at Frank. "By the way, this is my sister, Sarah. Sarah, Frank."

Sarah and Frank shook hands across the bar. "Very pleased to make your acquaintance Little Missy. As I can very well see with my own eyes, natural beauty runs deep in your family." He held her hand a moment longer than a hand shake and smiled at her.

"Well," Sarah started, "no wonder my sister speaks so fondly of you. You are quite an inspiration to a woman's ego."

"I only speak the truth. Only the truth. Hey Janelle, I believe Logan is downstairs. Want me to call him up?" Frank asked. He knew from hearing Logan talk about Janelle he had an emotional attachment to that lady. The fact that Janelle was here to see him confirmed to Frank she returned Logan's affection.

"Actually Frank, I would sort of like to surprise him. Can I go down?" She asked.

"Walk on, walk on. You are welcome anywhere. He is sitting down by the juke box, I believe." Frank was pouring the ladies each a diet soda.

Janelle thanked him, took a sip and looked toward the staircase. "Ok, I am off to surprise Logan with my presence and my new found freedom."

Janelle walked very cautiously down the steps. It was almost impossible to look down and so she felt for each step before taking it and held on to the handrail with a death grip. The bottom step finally arrived. Feet firmly on the floor, Janelle looked around, but didn't see Logan. She walked around the corner toward the jukebox and saw him. He had his back to her. She smiled and took a step toward him. Janelle took two more steps she saw a gorgeous and very tall young blonde woman walk gracefully into Logan's arms. She placed her head on his shoulder. He embraced her and placed his head on her shoulder. Janelle just stood there and watched them. Panic hit her, but she waited. The two of them just stood there holding each other.

Oh man, Janelle, this is awkward, she thought to herself as panic set in deeper. Janelle felt a lump forming in her throat.

The blonde started to step back out of Logan's embrace. It was really more of a long hug than it was an embrace or 'being held,' but Janelle was forced into jealousy and hurt seeing them together. To her, it was an embrace between lovers. As the blonde stepped back, she kissed Logan. A quick kiss, but Logan returned it. About that time a little blonde boy, maybe three or so, ran and grabbed Logan's leg. Janelle mentally shook her head to be sure she heard the small child's words as he spoke to Logan.

"Daddy, Daddy, pick me up," he sung out to Logan while dancing around at his feet.

Logan reached down and picked up the little boy. He pretended to toss him in the air and Janelle heard Logan speak. "Come here Jake. I sure love you little guy." Logan nuzzled the child's neck. Logan turned to the blonde and told her "I love you too, Kelly. I will always be here for you."

Janelle felt sick. How could she have completely misjudged Logan? How could he have told her how much she meant to him? He was married. He had a child. If he wasn't married then he still cared very much for the lady whose child he had fathered. Janelle backed up slowly and silently. She turned for the stairs. Tears fell hot down her cheek. She was an idiot. She was such an idiot. Sarah knew, she had to have known. That is why she pushed so much for Janelle to admit she didn't know Logan. Fear washed over her. She didn't want Logan to find her there. She did not want to be introduced to the people in his real life. She felt shattered.

Janelle came up the stairs as quickly as she could. Sarah turned smiling when she heard her. Sarah had expected to see Logan standing with her. Instead she saw Janelle crying as she sat at the first table at the top of the stairs.

"Honey, what happened?" Sarah was looking at Janelle expecting a physical injury from the stair climb.

"Get me out of here, Sarah." She mumbled as she sobbed quietly.

"What happened, Janelle?"

"Not here, I want to leave now, Sarah. Please let's go." Janelle was walking toward the door. She didn't see Frank as he walked back to the bar and saw them leaving.

"Ladies...," Frank started. Sarah turned and looked at him and gave him an "I don't know shrug" as she shook her head "no" in his direction. Janelle did not turn back or respond at all.

Outside Sarah again asked Janelle what had happened.

"Sarah," her voice was broken from the tears.

"Let's go. I'll tell you later." Her tears fell harder.

Neither saw the dark haired Mexican woman staring at them as she exited her truck. *Hmm,* she wondered to herself. *Wonder what the crew did to upset the cripple?* She kept walking toward the entrance.

Sarah closed Janelle's door and got in her side of the car. She started the car and drove off down the same road that had brought them here. Janelle was still crying and turned her body so she could look out the window. Sarah decided not to ask again. She would let Janelle bring it up when she was ready. Sarah's thoughts raced. Was Janelle down there long enough to have spoken to Logan?

Did he tell her his offer was a joke, was he not happy to see her? Was there someone there with him? "Oh no," Sarah though. She knew it would be the blonde. She should have told Janelle what she saw. She instantly hated herself.

CHAPTER TWENTY-EIGHT

"Kelly, is there anything I can say to make you change your mind?" Logan asked. He couldn't believe what she had just told him. Hadn't he lost enough this past three years? First his brother, his dad and now Kelly wanted to leave and take Jake away too. He would have no family left, except Carlos Mendoza who had always been like an uncle to him.

"Logan. I have thought this through. Did you know Dad left a letter for Frank to give to me in the event something happened to him?" She asked. Her eyes were tear filled. This was a tough thing she was doing, but it was the right thing to do. She just knew it.

"No," Logan answered so quietly that she wasn't sure he had even spoken at all. Logan put Jake down and he ran over to play with the trucks he had by the jukebox.

"I thought you knew. The reason I went to my sisters was because of that letter from your dad. The last piece of advice he could offer me, I guess. He must have known I have always let others make the decisions in my life, especially him since Patrick's death. He must have known

I would need some direction with him gone. I could not have loved him more if he had been my flesh and blood father." Kelly continued speaking to Logan, her eyes fixed on Jake playing. She started to say something else, but instead she broke into heavy tears and sobs. She picked up a cloth napkin from the table next to where they were standing and buried her face into it trying to control her emotions and trying not to let Jake know she was crying. Kelly turned her back to Logan. She knew that her tears upset him and she didn't want that.

Logan did not respond. He did not move toward her. He just let her talk. Whatever she was thinking and saying had to come out when she was ready. Whatever words she chose to share, and which ever ones she chose to keep in her heart, were being decided by Kelly as she spoke. Logan recognized the decision process. He recognized the 'time for me to grow up' indecision and realizing decisions had to be made for other people sometimes. The best support he could offer was to sit there and let her continue in her time.

Kelly's tears slowed to the point she could speak again. "The letter from Dad told me that he knew I had run away from my life when I came here and that since I married Patrick and had Jakey and stayed here, I was not handling my past. He told me how much family meant. How much I was hurt by Patrick's life and his death. He talked about how I had told him I felt like a fool because of Rachel. He talked about how I hated being called Patrick's widow and how the story always came with "the poor dear" attached. He told me that he had always tried to protect me from people's words, how much he loved me and how lost he thought I would be without him here. God, Logan, he was so right to know that." Kelly paused momentarily and glanced at him. She smiled, looked back at Jake and continued.

"Dad knew, Logan. He was so wise. Anyway, he told me to consider fixing things with my mom and sister. He told me to take a trip, go back there and just see them. He said I had a capacity to love that would overcome any hurt or problems. Also, that I am not nineteen anymore. I have been a wife, a good wife, and I am a mother. He told me he knew he could not tell me what to do and was actually posing an option that would be the hardest thing I ever had to do, go home to Michigan. He knew you would be hurt if I left, but he also said you would feel responsible to take care of me and Jake and that I would never find my own wings if I let you do that. He feared you would never find your own family if I made you care for Jake and I in a 'provider/father or husband' role instead of letting you be an uncle and brother in law." Kelly looked at Logan. She knew that part of the conversation would spark a comment.

"Kelly," he began, ready to disagree with everything she was saying.

Kelly held up her hand as it to stop his words.

"Don't disagree Logan. Just let Dad's words sink in. I know you would care for me and Jake. You shouldn't have to though. That's all."

Kelly walked over and took a knife away from Jake that he must have found on the floor. She turned and came back to Logan.

"Anyway. I have made up my mind. I want to go home to Michigan. I want to get to know my mom again and my sister. I want Jake to have a grandma to love him. I will make sure he comes back here for vacations and to spend summers because I want him to know all about you, Patrick and his Papa. Don't make this any harder Logan.

If you just look at me wrong I won't do this. It is what is right for me, for Jake and for Jake and me together. Okay?" She stopped and looked at him. Her eyes were red and puffy. To Logan she looked like a scared little girl.

Logan stood and looked at her. He turned his head and watched the tousle haired little boy that he loved like his own. He could not speak. He leaned forward and kissed Kelly's forehead. As he stepped back, he nodded to her and turned, without speaking and walked toward Jake.

Kelly watched Logan sit on the hearth around the fireplace and pick up one of Jake's cars. She needed to walk away and allow them their space alone together. Logan was dealing with his thoughts. She could not watch and think about taking Jake from Logan. She knew her decision was the right one. For once she felt in control of her life. It was hard, but Kelly loved the feeling. She turned to walk up the stairs to see Frank.

CHAPTER TWENTY-NINE

Rachel walked in and sat at the bar. The two men sitting at the bar looked at her and turned back to their conversation. No one thought much of Rachel, especially in the two years since Patrick's death.

One old man mumbled to the other "I can't believe that woman even comes in here." The other mumbled back, "it's because of women like her this town never needed a whore house."

"I can hear you. Do you mind?" Rachel snapped. They didn't even bother to look at her. The men just laughed loudly and went back to their drinking.

Frank walked up to Rachel. "What do you want here Rachel, I am sure you didn't come to socialize."

"I came to see my dad. Who upset the cripple I saw leaving here, you?" She snapped.

Kelly came up the stairs and Rachel saw her as she continued. "Perhaps it was you, Kelly. Did you upset the crippled girl and her friend?"

"Rachel shut up now," Frank warned in a low voice bordering on losing control. "You leave Kelly alone. I don't know what you saw out there, but I know that young lady and you are certainly not welcome to bad mouth her in my bar."

Kelly ignored Rachel. She certainly hated that woman.

"Where is my father, or Logan, either one?" Rachel really didn't want to talk to Logan, she just liked the reaction Kelly would have if she thought Rachel was going to talk to him. "Maybe I will go downstairs and find him." She was baiting Kelly as she rose and turned from her barstool.

Kelly stood and walked toward the staircase intentionally blocking the stairwell. "Rachel, Logan is busy right now. You need to leave him alone."

"How cute, Kelly. Moving on to the elder brother? I always did like him better of the two, but then your husband, well, he was an easy target." Her voice was venomous.

"THAT is it Rachel!" Frank was barely controlling the hatred and anger he felt. His face was flushing red as he came around the bar to see to it Rachel left. "Get the hell out of my bar!" Frank was standing beside her and grabbing her arm as she turned to leave.

"I'm going. Damn you are an uptight lot. Tell my precious padre I need to speak to him when you see him. Can you handle that?" She spat.

"Get. Out!" Frank's words were loud and firm. Rachel left.

Kelly was looking down at her hands and shaking her head. Logan had heard the last of the tirade from the stairs. That settled it in his heart. Kelly would always have to live down Patrick and Rachel's night together that caused his death. He came up the stairs with Jake and told Kelly it was time to leave. He wanted her out of there,

DEBBIE ISBELL

even though the people in the bar loved her.

CHAPTER THIRTY

Janelle finally turned in her seat to face her sister. With defeat in her voice she asked the question that Sarah knew would be coming. "You knew didn't you, that is what you were trying to tell me when I wouldn't let you finish, that he is married, and has a kid, wasn't it Sarah?" Janelle's tone was emotionless and held no accusation against her sister. She sounded defeated. This was a not a voice that Sarah was used to hearing come from her sister's mouth.

"Honey. I, I, well, please just tell me what happened in there. I did see Logan at the hospital with a blonde woman and a child." She spoke quietly. It was probably time to pull over and let Janelle walk and talk this out.

"I am such an idiot. I went downstairs and they were standing there. The happy little family. I saw him holding that blonde and the little boy called him 'Daddy," Janelle almost laughed as she spoke because of how stupid she had been to trust a man she never really knew. She figured what she said to Sarah had just about summed it up perfectly so she quit talking.

"Want me to pull over up here? We can breathe some fresh air?" Sarah posed both statements as questions. She wanted Janelle to choose.

"Let's stop. I don't know much about walking. My neck and head are killing me. Maybe we can find a stump or something close along the road." Janelle looked at Sarah as she spoke.

Sarah pulled off the road and they slowed to an area that was rather flat. There were some big boulder rocks and one looked the perfect height for Janelle to sit down with little effort or balance required.

"Jani, tell me what you saw or heard, besides the little boy calling him 'Daddy.' What did Logan say when he saw you?" She pressed gently.

"He didn't see me, Sarah. He had his back to me. I started to approach him and saw the woman walk into his arms. She rested her head on his shoulder and he tightened his arms around her. He told the little boy he loved him and then told her he loved her too. That was pretty much it. I turned and left." That was the whole encounter in a nut shell.

"Janelle, we don't really know the circumstance you know. I mean, the 'daddy' thing is hard to overcome, but, maybe they aren't involved." Sarah knew that was a stupid comment to make to her sister and was just about to say so when Janelle bit back.

"Decided to take his side now, huh? How did that happen?" Janelle closed her eyes wishing this entire day hadn't happened. The headache was throbbing in her temples, in the back of her skull and down into her neck and shoulders. The pain - both physical and emotional— caused Janelle's voice to be much more aggressive than she felt at that moment. She wanted to be anywhere but sitting in the car in the mountains of Flagstaff.

Sarah sat quietly. She would take Janelle back to the hotel and in the morning they would catch a plane back to Texas and Mitch would pick them both up at the airport. From that point things would move forward. Sarah was angry at herself for not protecting her sister better. She should have pushed Logan for an answer to the scene she saw. Janelle should never have had to face that reality.

CHAPTER THIRTY-ONE

Logan had kept Jake overnight. Kelly had wanted to go to the cemetery early Sunday morning. Logan figured it was either to tell Patrick her plans, forgive him, tell him he was a selfish ass, or all three and not necessarily in the order they were coming to him. Logan and Jake went to Shannon's Luck to have breakfast.

Carlos was there, as always cooking breakfast on Sunday morning. He came out with Jake and Logan's breakfast and Logan decided to confirm the cabin plans.

"You know Carlos, Janelle is supposed to be getting out of the rehab house next week. I would like to come and get the cabin ready, you know, stock it with food and all so she is ready to move in for the two months. I can tell she is going to stay. I will pay you for the two months. I just don't want her to know about it," Logan said quietly as if trying to make sure Janelle didn't hear him.

"No, no, Shannon," Carlos shook his head as he spoke. Carlos had always called him by the name Logan's father had given him. "I would not take money from you. That place usually sits empty. If I can make your lady's life a little easier, I will do it."

"Well," Logan began with a laugh in his voice, "She might not want to be called 'my lady', Carlos. She's a friend. I just want to do this for her."

"It will be done. You tell me when she will be there. I will ask my Lupita to fill the cupboards and provide clean linens and it will be perfect for her." Carlos smiled at Logan. He loved him like a son. Carlos dearly missed his friend, the senior Shannon Logan, and saw so much of the young man he had been in his son, and in his grandson as they sat there devouring their food.

CHAPTER THIRTY-TWO

Mitch and the Beckett's met the girls at the airport. Janelle's parents cried and held her. They were so glad she was home. They told her she should come stay with them. They would turn the study back into a bedroom for her. Janelle and Sarah told them everything was arranged, Sarah had the room and it was closer to Janelle's apartment.

"I plan on spending some time at my own place. I also hope to be able to live there alone in a few weeks once I am more comfortable in this brace," she announced to everyone. Janelle was very happy to see her family and to meet Mitch, but her heart was heavy with the disappointment at not being able to stay in Logan's life and in Arizona.

The family wanted to go to lunch, Janelle told them she was tired and was having serious headaches from the change in the brace. She wanted to go home, to Sarah's and rest.

"Honey you need to be sure to see a local doctor and start your care here as soon as possible, especially if those headaches continue," her father said gently, but with the expectation his daughter would listen to him as she had always done.

"Dad, the headaches and neck soreness are to be expected. I just haven't been taking the pain killers the doctor prescribed, I have been trying to take something over the counter," Janelle told him feeling loving warmth at being Daddy's little girl again if even just for a moment. "I promise to make an appointment this week. I have a copy of my records. Dr. Curtis told me he would contact the doctor on Monday and discuss my injury, my surgery and where I am in my recovery. I'll also be going back to Arizona in about three months to see Dr. Curtis. This is only the fourth time this surgery has been performed, it is still somewhat a miracle," Janelle said with humility. She certainly didn't take that fact for granted and she was very grateful God had spared her life. As it consumed her she could have been dead, tears filled her eyes. "I love you all so much. I certainly won't take you or my health for granted. I promise."

Her mother simply stepped forward and cradled her daughter against her chest. She knew it would be a long emotional recovery for Janelle and her mother would see to it that aspect was not forgotten.

Janelle kissed her mother on the cheek and then stepped back out of her arms. "And, speaking of health, Sarah, are you going to see a doctor about those dizzy spells you have been having?"

Sarah shot Janelle a look that said "What in the hell are you doing bringing that up in front of everyone?"

"Oh, it's nothing, but yes, I am going for a routine check-up. Don't worry, Mom, Dad or you Mitch, I've just been skipping breakfast and it's made me a little dizzy in the morning. I am going to see the doctor tomorrow as a precaution. Really, I'm fine," she announced laughing and hoping her family wouldn't make a bigger deal out of it than they should. Sarah was also hoping to convince herself she wasn't worried. The dizzy spells were now happening every morning the minute her feet hit the floor and were followed by a wave of nausea. She was not about to share that fact with anyone.

CHAPTER THIRTY-THREE

Monday morning Logan left Flagstaff to drive to see Janelle. He had missed her all weekend and had been so busy with Kelly and Jake and the ranch that he hadn't even had a chance to call her. Carlos and Lupita were angels about Janelle coming to stay. They would make everything right. They would fix up the downstairs room so that she had no reason to try and maneuver the stairs to the upper room. Once her halo brace was off and Janelle was able, Logan would make her at home in the loft too.

Logan arrived, parked his car and went inside. He walked into Janelle's room and saw the bed was made and the pictures and flowers were gone. *Hmm,* he was confused why Janelle wasn't in her room. *Guess they moved you.*

Logan walked to the nurses' station to find out what where Janelle was now.

"Mr. Logan, Ms. Beckett checked out Friday afternoon. She isn't here any longer," the nurse announced smiling because it was good news.

"Wow. I didn't know that," Logan sounded confused. "Thank you," he said as an afterthought. He turned and walked away not sure if the nurse was talking to him or had answered the phone. It didn't really matter at that moment. Why hadn't she called him? Or had she?

When Logan got outside he checked his phone for messages. There were none from Janelle. He called home, no messages there either. Logan decided he would call the hotel to see if Sarah and Janelle were there. He learned they had checked out yesterday morning he was told by the hotel attendant.

Logan went to his truck. "Now what?" He said as he sat there holding the steering wheel. He decided to call Frank. Maybe Janelle called there yesterday and maybe Frank had a message to give him when he got back. Frank hadn't known Logan was driving down to Phoenix today to see Janelle.

Logan called Frank from the parking lot of the hotel. The phone was answered on the second ring and a booming voice answered the phone that was all Frank. "Shannon's Luck, this is Frank, how can I help?"

"Frank, it's Logan," he announced, even though Frank knew that as soon as Logan spoke.

"Hello Son, what can I do for you?" Frank thought the world of Logan. He was a good boy. He never cared for Patrick, he had caused too much heartbreak for his friend Shannon Logan, but this boy; he was a keeper.

"Hey, I was wondering, did Janelle or her sister Sarah call the place at all yesterday? She isn't in rehab anymore. I thought maybe she would leave a message. I would like to know where she is before I drive back to Flagstaff." Logan sounded a little confused and a little ticked off although he tried to hide it. "I came down to Phoenix today to see her. She isn't here."

Frank was instantly confused and knew something was not right. "Logan, Janelle was here. Didn't you speak to her when she came downstairs Saturday?"

"Hell no, Frank. What the hell do you mean did I speak with her? No one told me she was there. When was she there? What did she say?" Logan's anger was almost out of check.

"Son, she wanted to surprise you. She was here Saturday a little before noon. She has her halo brace off and everything. I offered to call downstairs; you were down there with Kelly and Jake. Janelle insisted on surprising you," Frank softened his voice hoping to defuse the situation and calm Logan down.

"Damn it! What?" Logan was clearly angry. "Why didn't you say anything to me when you saw me later that day, Frank?"

"You know I mind my business when it comes to your family, Logan. Janelle came up the stairs crying and insisted her sister take her out of here. I tried to call after them and her sister just shook her head at me. Janelle didn't even turn around and they both left. Out of respect to both of you, I said nothing. Well, then Rachel showed up and my attention turned to protecting Kelly from her biting mouth. I expected Janelle had told you something you didn't want to hear. You were rather brooding when I saw you the rest of the day. I was respecting your privacy young man," Frank explained, but his tone of voice also said he had no intention of accepting any fault in this situation. He loved that boy, but if Logan thought he was sending any fault Frank's way, he was sorely mistaken.

Logan heard the tone in Frank's voice and it snapped

him out of the tantrum he wanted to have. Logan quickly remembered his manners. "I apologize Frank. I didn't know she came to Dad's. She never spoke to me while she was there. I don't know why she was upset. Perhaps she decided she wasn't staying in Flagstaff. Perhaps the memory of the accident hit her while she was back there. I don't know. I will call her. Thank you for the news. I will owe you when I get back up there for my bad attitude on the phone just now," Logan said apologetically. Frank thought he sounded both hurt and defeated.

"Dishes, you do a bar's worth of dishes, and I will call your bad attitude squared up." Frank was smiling and Logan could hear it in his voice. He was forgiven and felt relieved. He didn't want to ruin a lifetime long relationship with misplaced anger.

Logan laughed as he spoke. "I think you push people's buttons just to get your bar glasses washed, Frank."

"The towel and hot water awaits, young Logan." He smiled into the phone and then hung up laughing.

Logan smiled for a moment at Frank's laughter. It was short-lived. Logan knew he needed to call Janelle. It was Monday and almost noon. He had her sister's cell phone number, but of course, not with him. Logan would have to drive back to Flagstaff to call Sarah and get a contact number for Janelle. He missed Janelle and no matter what she had come to Shannon's Luck to tell him, Logan wanted to hear it. If Janelle wanted to tell him to pound sand, he would pound it, but the words had to come from her mouth. Logan left Phoenix and drove back to Flagstaff. While he drove his imagination ran rampant with what Janelle was there to tell him, none of it good.

. . . .

Sarah had again felt like total and complete death

warmed over when she woke on Monday morning. She called her doctor's office and they told her they had an 11:00 cancellation she could take. She did. The doctor was of course late for the appointment, but finally, she was able to see him.

Sarah explained what she had been feeling, what had been happening and what she thought was wrong.

"Well, let's take a blood test and see if anything is hiding there," the doctor told her. Her blood pressure was fine and the doctor had a thought. "Sarah, is it possible you are pregnant?"

Sarah laughed. "No, it isn't possible."

"Just asking. Your symptoms sound a lot like morning sickness. Let's do that blood test," he stated in that doctor voice that makes you sure if you weren't suffering from whatever the doctor just suggested when you arrived, you have it now.

"Oh, oh," Sarah said with a memory coming to her mind. "I suppose it is possible. Oh great. When will you have those results back?" Sarah panicked. This was not at all what she needed.

"I can call you before the end of the day. We do that test in house. If you are pregnant, I'll want to give you a prescription for prenatal vitamins and see you again in a month." He turned and walked out leaving her to digest what he had just willed into her life.

CHAPTER THIRTY-FOUR

It was almost noon now and Sarah wanted to see Mitch. She called to see if he wanted to have lunch and he readily accepted.

"What's wrong, Sarah?" Mitch asked worried when she was uncharacteristically quiet over lunch. "What did the doctor tell you when you were there today?"

"No news yet, he took blood. I am fine, fine." She was being intentionally evasive and Mitch knew it.

Mitch already suspected what Sarah would be telling him and what she was not telling him now. He decided to throw it out there and see if she was thinking the same thing or knew something she wasn't telling him.

"Sarah," Mitch said her name gently and then stopped talking. He waited for her to look at him. She did.

She looked like she was ready to cry. Mitch smiled lovingly and reached a hand across the table. Sarah took it. "You know I want to marry you don't you?"

Sarah nodded, smiled and squeezed Mitch's hand. She certainly knew she loved him. She just didn't want to tell him she was pregnant. She was a little excited, but not at the thought of losing him because he thought she trapped him. Not knowing what to say, she just sat there nervously waiting for him to continue.

"Good. I want to tell you something else. I know you want to wait a year or so to get married and that's fine if it's the right thing to do. Okay?" He said holding her hands and not looking away from her face.

"Yes Mitch." Sarah could not tell what was going on in his head. What he just said sounded like a precursor to something else. She felt like she was going to throw up and this was pure nerves.

"However," he paused and reached for her other hand. She gave it to him and smiled nervously. She took a deep breath and tried to calm down. "Sarah, if you are carrying my child, I won't wait to marry you." There it was out there now.

Sarah pulled both of her hands back out of his as if she had been burned. "What? Mitch, why do you think I'm pregnant?"

"Well, there is the obvious. We weren't very responsible that night. You are feeling dizzy and nauseated every day." He was smiling. "I am okay with all this by the way. Well, other than the fact we aren't married. Having a baby with you, Sarah, sounds perfect. I never thought I wanted kids, until this very moment."

Sarah sat back in her chair amazed at this man. He was reaching across the table, hands open to hold hers again. She just stared at him, hands in her lap.

"Why did God bring you to me, Mitch? Surely, I have never been good enough to deserve the gift you are to me. I will know if I am pregnant before the end of the day."

. . . .

Four o'clock finally came. So did the news. Sarah was pregnant. She hung up the phone in shock and panic. What in the world did she know about being a mother? She didn't even feed her cat every day! She had to call Mitch. No, she had to see Mitch.

Sarah went to his house and waited for him to come home. She was sitting on his porch, drinking an iced tea as he walked towards her smiling.

"Hi beautiful. Now this is a scene I could get used to. How are you?" He was asking "what did the doctor say?" without speaking those specific words. He had been anxious all day long. He realized as he stood there he would be disappointed if the doctor said they weren't having a baby. The thought caught him completely off guard.

Mitch pulled his porch chair in front of Sarah's and sat with his hands on her knees. He knew the answer. He could tell by looking at her, she was even more radiant than he ever thought her to be. "Tell me, Sarah," he whispered hopefully.

"Well, apparently everyone thought I was pregnant except me. Everyone was right. I am pregnant, Mitch." She looked at him and half smiled nervously. Mitch pulled her close and hugged her.

"I so completely love you Sarah Beckett. Please marry me. Now," Mitch whispered into her ear as he held her. When he sat back he pulled a small box out of his pocket and handed it to her. He pushed the chair back and knelt down to one knee. Sarah began to cry.

"Sarah. I know this relationship has happened very fast. We seem to be on a fast track. You know something, it's the right track though. We are meant to be. You, me and obviously a little one too. Please, Sarah. Please.

Marry me. Marry me soon." He just stared at her smiling and excited and hopeful.

"Oh Mitch," Sarah took the ring box and stared at the ring. "Are you sure?" She asked giggling with tears running down her cheek.

"No, Sarah, I was just joking! Of course! I am completely sure. Marry me tomorrow, Sarah. If not tomorrow, then this weekend." He was standing and laughing as he pulled her up.

"Yes, Mitch, yes. I will marry you. Well, we will marry you," she said looking down at her still flat stomach. She could not wait to tell Janelle and her parents she was getting married. The baby on the other hand, that was a tale she wasn't looking forward to telling her parents. "I need to tell Janelle. She is going to be so surprised!"

The two agreed to have dinner at Sarah's and invite her parents to tell them they were getting married. Janelle would hear about the baby as soon as Sarah got home. Her parents would not. They talked awhile longer and agreed that the wedding would be in one month. Quick, too quick for Sarah, not quick enough for Mitch. This would allow time to plan a small wedding.

As Sarah was leaving Mitch's house her cell phone rang. She didn't recognize the number and decided to let it go to voice mail.

CHAPTER THIRTY-FIVE

No answer. Logan decided to leave a message. "Hi Sarah. It is Logan. Logan from Arizona. I went to see Janelle today and they told me she was out of rehab. I wasn't aware she was out. I'm really happy Janelle is out. I also heard they took off her halo brace. I bet she is thrilled." He decided not to say anything about the incident at Shannon's Luck, he would let Sarah or Janelle explain. "I don't have a number for Janelle other than yours. Can you have her call me please or call me back and give me her number. Thanks. Hope your family is fine." He hung up. He had a bad feeling. He hoped he was imagining the worst.

CHAPTER THIRTY-SIX

"Janelle," Sarah called as she came in, dragging her name out as if carrying a note in a song. "Oh, sister dear, where are you?"

"In the kitchen, Sarah," Janelle called back with far less enthusiasm than her sister.

"So, guess what?" Sarah was beaming as she began the guessing game with her sister.

"You won the lottery." Janelle was still unhappy and still nursing a sore neck and relentless headache. Her voice told this, but Sarah would not let it ruin her moment.

"Wrong, guess again," Sarah teased.

"Honey, do we have to do this?" Janelle asked with a weariness in her voice. She could hear her sister's excitement and felt horribly mean, but she just couldn't play the happy sister right now.

"No, you don't have to guess." Sarah's voice lost just a touch of the enthusiasm she had been exuding a moment ago. "Feel like talking a minute? I really want to share something with you." Sarah sounded so hopeful and happy, it caught Janelle's attention and she finally realized she needed to stop moping and play the game with her sister.

"I guess that...," Janelle began, sounding much more jubilant, for Sarah's sake, than she actually felt. "Let's see. That you...," just that second she saw the diamond ring on Sarah's hand. "Oh, Sarah," she exclaimed and grabbed her hand. "My guess is that Mitch proposed!!" She stood up and reached over to quickly hug Sarah without even allowing her to answer.

Emotional as sisters can always be, happy tears formed in both of the girls eyes. Janelle loved hugging her sister. Sarah was giggling. "Janelle, I have to tell you a secret."

Janelle pulled back so she could see her sister's face and said "You didn't get married this afternoon did you? Oh, I will be so mad if you don't have a proper wedding so I can wear a stunning dress and be your Maid of Honor," she laughed as she spoke. Janelle's mood had instantly improved and her painful neck and head were all but forgotten, at least temporarily.

"No, no, Jani, we didn't get married this afternoon. We want to get married in about a month," Sarah stated knowing Janelle would comment and then she would tell her why.

"A month? Oh no, that will absolutely not work! How can we plan a wedding in a month? I want to be out of this damn neck brace and wearing a slinky, gorgeous, brilliantly colored dress. A month will never do. Why don't you get married in October? October is a beautiful month to get married, well as long as you don't make us wear costumes like a Halloween party or something." Janelle was planning and planning. She was genuinely happy, and completely ignored the sad voice in the back of her head whispering to her how much she desperately wanted to marry Logan. She started to speak again about flowers and the church when Sarah cut her off and stopped her dead in her tracks with one statement.

"Janelle, I'm pregnant." Sarah looked at Janelle and held her breath waiting for her sister's response.

Janelle sat down realizing she just misheard her sister. "Say that again, Sarah," Janelle spoke quietly.

"I'm pregnant. Mitch is thrilled. Turns out he already suspected as much. I went to his house to tell him and he proposed to me. Ring and all." Sarah held her hand out so they could both examine the brilliant diamond on her left hand. "I said yes," she proclaimed as if Janelle were waiting for the end of the story.

"Of course you did, silly." Janelle stood and hugged Sarah. "My goodness, I'm going to be an aunt. Auntie Janelle, I like it. When are you going to tell Mom and Dad?"

"Well, we are doing this piece meal. We are going to tell the folks tonight. They've been invited for dinner. Mitch is grabbing ready-to-serve Italian. As for the baby, that news will wait until after we're married. I think they would be too disappointed in me to enjoy the marriage announcement. I know that they'll figure it out, but at least we can enjoy the evening and the wedding and then when the time is right, I will tell them. Then they can enjoy the idea of being grandparents too." Sarah had it all figured out.

"Okay, good idea, Sis. We'll have to dress shop immediately. I know just the perfect little wedding dress shop. It is family owned, a mother and her daughter. I went there with a co-worker several months ago. They are perfect there." Janelle would see to it that the plans came together as quickly as Mitch and Sarah figured out where, how big and what the color scheme was to be. She hugged her sister. "Well, if we are having a celebration. I best go shower. I will yell if I need help okay?" Off she went to the bathroom with a feeling of happiness she was thrilled to have overwhelming her life. Logan was temporarily forgotten.

Sarah remembered the voice message on her phone and decided to check it. She put in her PIN number and heard Logan's voice. She listened to the message and was instantly irritated with Logan acting as if everything were fine. Did he truly think they just forgot to tell him where Janelle was or that she had been released? Sarah knew Janelle didn't need to know Logan called and they didn't need to explain anything to him. He should've been above board with Janelle and he was not going to get the opportunity to back pedal now. Sarah deleted the message. Logan had said he had no other way to get in touch with Janelle. It would stay that way.

Dinner was a huge success. Her parents were thrilled and only envisioned a quick wedding because the two were so in love and hated being apart. They completely approved and everyone sat and planned the wedding. It would occur in exactly two days shy of a month on a Saturday evening at Sarah's parents' church. Mitch and Sarah agreed to visit Mitch's mom and dad and tell them the next evening. He would call the twins. They would be elated. It was agreed between Sarah and Mitch that the baby news would wait.

"First weekend in June it is." Everyone toasted. No one noticed that Sarah did not drink her wine. Mitch switched glasses with her to make it look as if she participated in the wine festivities during dinner.

"This weekend we go dress shopping Mom and Sarah," Janelle announced. Her sister, a bride. What a beautiful one she would be.

CHAPTER THIRTY-SEVEN

Three days had gone by and Logan's mood had not gotten any better. He wasn't sleeping, wasn't much use around the ranch or the office, and Kelly found him positively grumpy when he was helping her pack. She was leaving that weekend and the movers were expected Friday to get her belongings. Jake would be back for the summer, a fact he couldn't understand and one Logan hated, but would never voice.

"Logan," Kelly began, "call her again. Maybe she missed the number and tried to call, but didn't get it right." She sounded encouraging.

"Kelly, that's very sweet, but we both know it is bullshit. Janelle knows how to reach Carlos and she knows the name of Dad's place. If she wanted to reach me, she would. Something happened, I just don't know what," he said with a frustrated tone. "Just let it be. If the woman doesn't want me, she doesn't want me."

"Call her, Logan," Kelly insisted. "Please call her."

Logan sat doing nothing and felt Kelly staring at him for at least five minutes. "Fine. I will." Logan announced and walked out into the courtyard to place the call.

Once again there was no answer. He hung up and dialed again. This time the phone answered immediately. He suspected it had not rung on the other end.

"Hello." It was Sarah. "Hello?"

"Don't hang up, please Sarah, its Logan," he said quickly with guilt looming in his voice.

"Hello Logan. What do you want? Please don't say it's my sister." She was impatient with him, but didn't hang up. Logan took that as a good sign.

"Care to tell me why Janelle ran crying from

Shannon's Luck and never spoke to me while you two were there? Care to tell me why she was there is the first place?" He sounded a little impatient himself.

"Oh Logan, don't play coy, it does not become you and Janelle deserves so much better than that. Just leave her alone. Acting as if you don't know what is going on, Logan, is childish and wrong." Sarah was pissed and she did nothing to curb the anger in her voice.

"Just tell me Sarah. I really, really don't know." He almost sounded believable, but Sarah was not falling for the naive routine when it came to her sister.

"Logan. Ask you wife and child. Perhaps they can explain to you why it is wrong to lead my sister into believing you cared for her romantically all the while being completely unavailable. Ask them. I just bet your wife will even agree with Janelle that you are a complete ass," Sarah was yelling.

"Hold the hell on a minute, Sarah. I am not married," Logan yelled back.

"Bullshit, Logan. Janelle saw you with your wife and heard your son call you 'daddy.' Leave us alone. You are not welcome any longer in our lives. Thank you for what you did, even though your intentions are still unclear to me. Just leave my sister alone. You have done her more harm than good playing her like this." Sarah hung up and heard Logan speaking as she did.

"Sarah just let me talk to Janelle...," The line was dead. He slammed the phone down and pounded his fist into the table. "Damn it," he yelled and took off walking into the woods.

Logan walked for forty-five minutes. He decided to sit and stare into the woods for relief. He was brainstorming on how to fix this whole mess and how he was going to get to Janelle and make her listen. He heard a whimpering that was fairly close. He got up and went to investigate. He walked toward a stream and saw what looked like a soaking wet pillow case. The case looked like it had a rock around it. He knew immediately there would be a dog in that damned case. Someone had tried to drown the pup, but the creek had not risen enough to do the trick.

"Bastards," Logan mumbled. It seemed nothing was going to improve his demeanor today. He untied the bag and out popped the smallest little brindle colored pup he had ever seen. It could only have been four or five weeks old. A runt looking thing to him, but it was alive, and Logan felt like caring for it.

Logan picked up the little dog he affectionately called "mutt" and it began to lick his face. It certainly smelled of puppy breath and Logan laughed. Puppy breath appeared to be the treatment for his foul mood. He walked back to dad's house, his house now, and set the puppy in the middle of the boxes and paper Kelly had in the living room. Jake squealed with excitement and tried to hug it.

"Careful fella, it's a tiny baby," his mother said. She

looked inquisitively at Logan.

"Found it in the stream. Someone was trying to kill it," he announced. "Guess it's mine now. You better name it, Jake." He walked to the kitchen to get some milk for the little guy, or gal, he corrected himself.

When he walked back with milk and a piece of bread in it Jake was sitting on the floor with the puppy on his lap. Apparently it had a name. He heard Jake saying "nice Bandy, nice Bandy." Logan looked at Kelly.

"Jake said that Papa loved Brandy. He wants to call it after "the girl Papa loved." Sound good to you?" She laughed. Logan and Kelly knew that Papa loved his Apricot or Peach Brandy, and it came in a bottle.

"Brandy it is," Logan stated. Jake took the puppy out back and Logan and Kelly went back to packing. She had heard him swear and yell and then watched the determination and anger in his walk as he left the courtyard. She knew that walk all too well. He had done the exact same thing the same night they were all having dinner and Sheriff Kyle came to the door to tell them that Patrick had been killed when he drove his truck off the mountain side. That night Logan swore and walked out. He was gone for hours.

He dealt with things his own way, especially grief, well his grief she thought. She decided not to ask what happened on the phone call. Obviously it wasn't good.

CHAPTER THIRTY-EIGHT

Saturday came way too fast for Logan. Kelly was exuberant and pleased with her decision. Her mother had been thrilled when she heard the news. Kelly had not spoken to her sister, but her mother told her they both could not wait for her to come home. Her mother cried at the thought of finally getting to see her precious little grandson she had not even met yet.

"Well, Logan. It looks like I have done all I can here. It's time for me to get to the airport. It's going to seem strange walking out that door. This has been my home for four years now. I love it here," she smiled while she talked even though her eyes were tear filled. Jake came running in with the puppy in his arms.

"Can I take Bandy Mama?" He was begging with his eyes and his heart. The timing on this pup showing up was bad for Jake.

"No Jakey, he is Uncle Logan's puppy. When you come to visit Uncle the puppy will be here and will be bigger so it can play with you. When we get settled at Grandma's house we will see about getting you your own puppy there, ok?" *Great Kelly, just keep adding on the heartbreak for this child*, she thought to herself.

"Dog's don't fly partner," Logan said and took the puppy from Jake. "I will put him in his kennel and meet you both in the car." Logan turned and walked away.

***

It seemed like the hours flashed by before Jake and Kelly got on the plane. Logan fought begging them to stay. They were his family. He had long since thought about how well his father knew them and the wisdom in leaving that letter for Kelly, so he didn't ask her to stay.

"I love you two, don't forget that. Take care of your mama Jake. Be good for her and your Gramma. Get going, you'll miss your plane," he said choking back a wall of emotion. "I will see you in a few months, bet you will have grown a foot by then." He tousled Jake's hair and leaned in to hug Kelly. She grabbed on to him and was shaking with the control it was taking for her not to cry.

"Ask me not to go Logan and I will stay," she whispered.

"Don't miss your plane, Kelly. Don't miss your plane." A tear slid down his cheek and he quickly pushed it away with his hand. "I will always be here."

Jake and Kelly boarded the plane. Logan stood there and watched the boarding hall until they closed the door. He felt a door in his heart slam shut too. Then he stood and watched the plane until he saw the big bird leave the ground and its wheels pull in. They were on their way and would call when they arrived.

Logan walked to his car, paid the airport parking fee and started home. It was a long drive from Phoenix to Flagstaff he thought. Janelle's face hit his memory like a ton of bricks.

When Logan pulled in to Shannon's Luck he was tired and all he thought of was a strong drink, or three. This month was causing him to hurt, and he hated that feeling.

Logan walked into the bar and the bartender—an old man Logan had known since he was a small boy and one who never kept his thoughts to himself - shouted over to him.

"Logan, you look like you were drug through a sticker bush backwards!" He laughed and went back to his beer commenting to his drinking buddy about how funny he was.

Frank poured Logan a whiskey and stood there with the bottle. He knew that first one would be gone in a gulp and it was. He poured him another. "You know the old man isn't wrong Logan. You really need to take care of yourself, son. I know with your pa and the thing that happened with Janelle and now Kelly and Jake leaving you must feel like someone is cutting out your soul with a dull knife, but you have to live and you have to live strong, son. Today is a dark day, but it will get better." Frank touched Logan's shaking hand. Logan held tight to the shot glass of whiskey in front of him.

"Too much at once, Frank. Way too much at once. For tonight I am going to get good and drunk, crash downstairs in the office when you toss me down the stairs, and tomorrow I will get it together. Deal?" He was spent and Frank knew it.

"Okay, Son." Frank left the bottle sitting next to him and watched him pour and drink. Frank would take care of him. He, Shannon, and Carlos had helped mend that boy's heart when his ma died, again when his brother died, and Frank would do it now. Logan wasn't one to give his heart away to undeserving people. He had faith this would work out. It just needed the right time.

After Logan had polished off four or five shots, he was feeling the loose tongue effects of the alcohol. He was in a safe place and he was hurting. Logan decided to voice his questions out loud. Frank was a bartender, he would know the answers. That was his job.

Logan asked one question and then kept asking questions without waiting for an answer. "Frank, why the hell does Sarah think I am married? Why would she tell Janelle that? What the hell is wrong with those women thinking I would cheat on my wife if I had one? Doesn't Janelle know me better than that after I sat by her damned bedside for all that time? Do you think she is married and trying to ditch me? What do you think, Frank? Huh? What should I do? What would you do?" He was hurting and the alcohol wasn't making the pain subside.

"Why don't you call her again, Logan? Not tonight, but tomorrow. You said you know her parents' names. Look them up, call them and have them call her or give you the number," Frank suggested. He knew there was a special reason Janelle had come to the bar. He had no idea what spooked her. "Women sometimes don't need a real reason, Logan. She may have misunderstood something she heard or saw."

"Call the Beckett's, that's what I will do. That woman is going to listen to me if I have to turn her over my knee and hold her there!" Logan slammed his shot glass down a little too hard on the bar. He knew then it was time to quit. "I am going downstairs, Frank," he announced.

Frank walked with him. He certainly did not want Logan falling down the damned stairs and breaking his neck. He knew Logan was going to feel bad in the morning.

As Logan tried to get comfortable on the couch in the office he vaguely recalled Frank's words and a feeling washed over him that Janelle had seen him with Kelly and Jake. He didn't stay awake long enough to pursue the line of thought.

CHAPTER THIRTY-NINE

The wedding dress shopping had been perfect. Sarah scheduled to go in for an initial fitting the following week. The dress was the color of ivory. She felt that best given her current situation. It was made of satin and hung slinky and straight with a plunging neck line. The cap sleeves were all lace with tiny glass beads throughout the lace. The same tiny glass beads were all across the bust and bodice. The back had buttons from the top all the way down past where the dress would hit Sarah's bottom. The back bunched at the waist as the extra material in the dress began to flow down and out into a short three foot train. The train had the same beadwork as the bodice of the dress. It was stunning. Sarah decided not to wear a veil. She tried on over a dozen and they all felt wrong. Her mother said tiny flowers and beads that made a halo would be beautiful or that pulled part of her hair off her face with scattered flowers throughout. They decided there was time to figure that out later. Sarah made a mental note to see her hairdresser in the next week. Sarah was stunning in the dress. She looked like and angel in white. She told her mother and sister how silly she felt in the very formal gown.

"I feel like I am playing dress up." She had a certain sadness that Janelle could not put her finger on. Lori, the store owner, and the fitting woman, Sandy, knew this look. It was the look of a woman who did not want to really be the center of attention and who did not want to look stupid in the wrong gown. They had been here hundreds of times a week.

"It is my plan to take you from a woman playing dress up to a bride, Sarah," Lori said smiling at her. "This dress was made for you. Next time you try it on you will feel more comfortable in it. When you try it on after your fitting, you will see yourself and feel like a bride. I promise you that!"

The sisters and their mother had a group hug with Lori and Sandy. Everyone was happy. It was time to go look at announcements, color schemes and flowers. They were making a day of it. This was partially because they were having so much fun and partially because they had so little time.

CHAPTER FORTY

Sunday morning came around and Logan's first thought was that he would never drink again. He sat up and put his feet on the floor of the office. He didn't try to stand. The room started to spin. He decided to just sit there and stare down at the floor for a few minutes. When he didn't feel better he closed his eyes. "Dumb ass," he said to himself.

Slowly the fog began to clear and Logan stood and went to the window. One thought washed over him as he stood there. If he was right, then Janelle had every reason to think he was married and be upset with him. He had to reach Janelle and make sure she knew this was wrong. If that is what she saw, he could fix it. If it was something else, he would damned sure fix that too, but she had to talk to him. He went upstairs to have some coffee, his stomach was not quite ready to eat, although he knew in very short order he would be ready to 'carbo load' his system to feel better. For some reason he was feeling encouraged by his realization and just a little ticked off Janelle didn't trust him enough to confront him before jumping to conclusions.

Logan knew that tomorrow morning the cattle round up would begin. He knew that he had to be there and be productive. He had over 50,000 head of cattle that had to be located, rounded up and moved to summer grazing land. This would be a tough week, but it was one that Logan always loved. A week on horseback would be just what he needed to work out the issues in his life. Whether it was a conscious decision or not, Logan would ride out his father's death, Kelly and Jake leaving, and this unresolved issue with Janelle. When he returned, he would be a whole man and able to handle his world again. He decided to make one more call to Sarah. He would tell her what he thought, what the truth was and that he was not reachable for a week. He would beg, although she would not know it, for Janelle to call him Monday next.

He dialed the phone. He knew Sarah would not answer when she saw the Arizona "928" area code.

"Hi Sarah. It's Logan again. Please listen to this message. Please ask Janelle to listen to this message. I have a feeling Janelle saw me downstairs hugging my sister-in-law. Her name is Kelly. My nephew's name is Jake. She was telling me she was leaving town. This has been a rough time for us, with Dad dying and all. My brother died two years ago. I am all Jake has now. Anyway. I guess what I want, well, what I need you to know, is that I am not married. I am not involved in a romantic relationship with Kelly and I am not Jake's father even though he sometimes calls me "daddy." I have a cattle round up this week. I will not be reachable by telephone. I really need to talk to you Janelle. If you want to be left alone, then be the woman I know you are and tell me yourself, please, that is all I ask. I just need you to know I...,"

BEEP "...*love you.*" He finished the sentence anyway.

He knew that Janelle wouldn't hear the last part. It was okay though because Logan planned to tell Janelle himself next Monday when he got back from the ride.

Logan left, he needed to check and make sure the cattle trucks were present and that they had more coming each day. This was a costly endeavor, with the extra hired hands they needed, two eighteen wheelers a day for a week, and then the stragglers had to be located and driven down in the twenty foot cattle trailer they kept at the ranch, or rounded up in a corral until another rig could be scheduled. This is what Logan loved best about being a rancher. It was what he did best. Running the ranch was a family necessity. Being the boss and owner was his position in the family. Being one of the guys and working as a team was what made him feel alive.

***

Sarah heard Logan's message that afternoon. She hadn't decided what to do about it. She just felt that it was too much trouble for Janelle. She decided not to tell her the truth. She would call Logan on Monday and tell him that Janelle didn't want to talk to him and ask him to please respect that fact and leave her alone.

CHAPTER FORTY-ONE

Monday rolled around. The wedding plans were perfect. As previously planned, Sarah dialed Logan's number early in the morning. It went straight to voice mail just as she had hoped.

"Hi Logan, I hoped if I waited until today I would catch you in person." She did not mean that, but she didn't want to be completely evil as she already sported much guilt from the decision to make this call. "I wanted to call and tell you Janelle heard your message. She really doesn't want to do this. She wants you to leave her alone. I don't know if she believes your story or not about Kelly and Jake, but it doesn't matter. She won't be calling to tell you herself. Please leave her alone, Logan, she is still recovering and I don't want you to upset her. Good luck to you Logan." Sarah hung up. She felt as if she had just committed a horrible crime.

***

Logan received the message on Monday. His words were choice. He reached down and patted Brandy's head. "This isn't over girl, not by a long shot. Janelle has too much in her to not tell me herself. Something is just not right."

Logan had a plan to buy some horses in Texas. He made an instant decision that he would have them delivered by train from Houston to Abilene and he would drive there himself to pick them up. While he was there, he was going to call on Janelle Beckett. She could tell him in person that he needed to butt out of her life. If she did, he would accept it. No other way though, no other way.

CHAPTER FORTY-TWO

Janelle could not believe that it had been a month. She loved the dress she was going to wear. It was a desert rose colored dress. Strapless with a slight train, about a foot or two behind her. She would carry pink roses. Her sister had Calla lilies and roses. It would be perfect. Even more perfect was the fact that Dr. Ross agreed she could take off her brace for the ceremony and pictures. Her promise was that she would be properly escorted down the aisle ahead of Sarah. Mitch's brother, Daniel, would walk with her and understood how important it was that she not trip or fall. She felt like a princess when she put that dress on. True to the promise of Lori in the bridal shop, Sarah had announced to everyone as she cried in happy tears, that she felt like a beautiful bride when she saw herself yesterday in her finished gown. She was brilliant.

Janelle and Sarah had been to the hairdressers at 11:00 and now it was 3:00. Daniel was going to pick Janelle up at 5:30 to drive her to the church. There was nothing to do, but wait. Sarah sat and admired her nails, her hair, and the necklace she would put on just before the ceremony. Nothing could ruin this day, especially since Sarah was no longer feeling sick in the morning.

Janelle waited. Patience was something she was getting much better at, but she still fidgeted like a small child.

CHAPTER FORTY-THREE

Logan had talked to the Beckett's earlier that morning before he made it to town. He decided to call them just on the whim that they didn't know about the issue between himself and Janelle. And, the possibility he was right about Sarah being involved somehow. He was right. They were all too pleased to hear from him and gladly gave him Janelle's home number when he told them he wanted to call her before he left town.

Now, here he was, sitting outside her house. He just needed to go knock. He looked at Brandy sleeping on the seat next to him. He looked at himself in the rear view mirror. "This might be ugly girl," he said to Brandy as he tousled her ears. She whimpered at him and he knew it was her way of telling him he was the most incredible man in the world and not to worry because Janelle was going to throw herself into Logan's arms the minute she saw him. *"Easy there Logan. Don't fall into a fantasy conversation just yet."*

Logan walked up to the door and rang the doorbell. It was 4:30 p.m. He didn't know about Sarah's wedding so he was surprised when Janelle answered the door in a stunning gown with her hair in curls, and she looked thrilled to see him, or did she?

Janelle's smile faded. "Logan?" That was all she said. She was expecting Daniel, figuring he had come early and her wait would be over. Never in a hundred years did she expect to see Logan. She was not ready for the sight of him standing there and it showed. She looked as if someone had punched her in the stomach and all her wind had left her body.

"Hi, I know, I know you didn't want to see me again, Sarah told me, but - Janelle, I needed you to tell me you didn't believe me for yourself. So here I am." He looked her in the eye and would not waiver from her stare.

"Logan? What are you talking about and why are you here?" She sounded a little angry. "My sister is getting married in two hours. I don't have time for this right now. I haven't heard from you in over a month. You can't just show up here now."

"I left messages with your sister, Janelle. I explained everything to her. She said you didn't want to talk to me. I tried to contact you." He suspected Janelle knew nothing after she left Shannon's Luck in tears. He blamed Sarah, but would not attack the sister at this point in the conversation. "Let me come in and talk to you for thirty minutes. If after that you want me to go, I will go."

Janelle stood and looked him in the eye for a minute or more, her heart and mind were running in every direction. She wanted to throw herself into his arms and thank God he was there. She wanted to cuss him out and tell him to get the hell off her porch. She opted for somewhere in between. She looked over his shoulder and saw the small puppy standing in the window of his truck. That made her smile.

"Back up?" She asked as she tipped her head in the direction of his truck referring to his puppy.

Logan looked back and saw Brandy looking out the window at him. He smiled too. "Just a little runt I saved from drowning. She is a feisty little lass," he stated as he turned back at Janelle.

Her features and her heart softened at his words. He had saved her, maybe not from the crash, or drowning, but he was there when she wanted to drown in darkness and give up. He would not allow that to happen. She loved him.

"Get your dog and come in Logan. I want to hear what you have to say," Janelle's voice as she spoke was tender and Logan felt elated at the sound of it.

He retrieved Brandy from the truck and made the introductions. Logan and Janelle sat down at the kitchen table and the puppy played on the tile floor. She waited for him to start.

"Thank you for being you, Janelle." He touched her hand.

"Logan, we have a lot to figure out before you thank me for anything." She looked intent. She was willing to listen and to be fair. She knew somehow Sarah had been instrumental in blocking their contact. She would give Logan the benefit of that doubt.

"I heard you came to see me at Dad's. I also heard you left crying. I've tried to reach you. I went to see you at the hospital and found you had been discharged. I found out after that, only after that, you had been at Dad's. Then when I was drunk Frank said something to me and I realized there must have been a horrible misunderstanding and I needed to correct it." Logan was speaking quickly. He didn't want Janelle to cut him off, he needed her to know the truth so she would no longer hurt or doubt herself or him.

"Anyway," he continued. "I'm not married, Janelle. The blonde is my sister-in-law. The boy is my nephew...," he told the whole story. He explained about Rachel and Patrick and how that all ended. He talked for thirty straight minutes.

When he finished everything he could think to tell her, he looked at her. She just stared at him. Her face gave nothing away. After three or four minutes, the longest silent time Logan had ever spent, Janelle sighed, she stood up and kept looking at him. Her heart told her to trust this crazy man in front of her who was willing to risk being emotionally kicked in person just to tell her the truth. He didn't give up on her when she was dying or now. He deserved her trust. She wanted him in her life. She smiled at him and crossed the three or four steps to where he was sitting. She stood there, looking down at him from that close the best she could with a brace on.

"Logan, I believe you," she whispered. "I do not doubt you. I am sorry about Sarah, she was probably trying to protect me. I believe you."

Logan stood and enveloped her in his arms. He inhaled her hair and just stood there. This was a perfect moment. He never wanted to let her go.

The doorbell rang. It was Daniel this time. She explained to Logan about Daniel and the wedding and then to Logan about the wedding. She asked Logan to go with her to the wedding. He complained about nothing to wear as he was here to buy cattle. She looked disappointed and the look on her face made him willing to do anything she wanted.

"I suppose there is a clothing shop somewhere close to here that I could get some wedding type duds. This isn't black tie for guests is it?" He asked with a song in his voice that he had not felt for eons.

"Well, the mall is close. They have men's clothing stores. I have to go with Daniel, but you could meet us there. Will you really get clothes? Oh, Logan I would love you to be there. That would be so perfect, you there as Sarah and Mitch start their new life together and you and I - well, we start over, right?" Janelle was so happy.

"You get your gorgeous behind to the wedding. I will sit and behave until after the wedding. By the way you look amazing. I can't believe how beautiful you are Janelle. I need directions and a church name and I will be there on time." Logan was glad he had chosen to shower and comb his hair before coming to Janelle's house.

***

Janelle and Daniel arrived at the church. She immediately checked in with Sarah who was in her dress and finishing the touches on her make up.

"Oh, Sarah," Janelle exclaimed. "You are so beautiful. You are absolutely radiant." Janelle was beaming and had color in her cheeks that Sarah had not seen in years. Then it hit her.

"He's in Abilene isn't he?" Sarah asked with a guilt filled voice.

Janelle hugged her. "I forgive you. I love him and he told me everything. He is coming to the wedding. Be happy for me, please, Sarah."

"I am happy for you sis, very happy." Sarah decided now was not the time to discuss why she did what she did. She knew that it would have to be discussed sometime in the future, but not today. Today was to be perfect for Sarah and for Janelle.

The ceremony finally began. Music played. Janelle kissed Sarah and then removed her neck brace. Sarah put the necklace around Janelle's neck. Then Janelle carefully, very carefully, stepped outside the room and took Daniel's waiting arm.

Soon the Pastor and Mitch walked to the front of the church from the left side foyer. Mitch was handsome in his tuxedo. He looked terrified, but Janelle knew that was to be expected.

The flower girl and ring bearer, both in white, walked to the front of the church. They were perfect. The sweet little flower girl was the daughter of a co-worker of Sarah's. She dropped pink rose petals perfectly as she walked.

Next, Mitch's brother and a friend of Sarah's from work walked to the front. It was soon Janelle and Daniel's turn. As she stepped into the church she saw Logan sitting on her right. He was wearing a dark blue suit with a white shirt and blue/grey paisley tie. He took Janelle's breath away. Logan knew it and smiled as she watched him. Janelle and Daniel walked to the front of the church. Daniel did not leave her arm and part as the others had at the end of the silk carpet. He walked her to her place at the front of the church and then walked to his place by Mitch.

The wedding march began. Sarah and Mr. Beckett walked slowly into the church and up the silken aisle to the front of the church. A tear ran down Janelle's face as she saw her beautiful sister living her dream come true in marrying her prince. Janelle glanced at Mitch. His eyes were fastened on Sarah's and he was smiling from ear to ear. Sarah was smiling back and a tear was sliding down her cheek. No one ever knew that a 30 foot hall could be so long.

The ceremony was beautiful. Mitch and Sarah had written their own vows which fit them perfectly. There was not a dry eye in the room. Mitch and Sarah lit the Unity Candle from the two individual candles sitting beside it. For being pulled together so quickly, this wedding was fairytale perfect.

The Pastor announced that Mitch and Sarah were husband and wife. He told Mitch he could kiss his bride and he did. The newly married couple turned and the Pastor announced them for the first time as Husband and Wife.

"Ladies and gentleman, allow me to introduce to you for the very first time, Mr. & Mrs. Mitchell Hansen."

Cheers and clapping erupted throughout the church and then the recession music began and the wedding party exited just as perfectly as they entered. Daniel held tight to Janelle's arm. Logan was waiting as she exited the church. He kissed her gently on the cheek as she stepped from Daniel's arm to his. He leaned in closer as she moved into his embrace. Logan whispered in her ear as she hugged him. "I want to be next, Janelle. Please marry me."

Janelle pulled back quickly. She was startled by what she just heard. She wasn't sure she had heard him correctly. He smiled at her and winked. At that very moment Sarah and Mitch came through the door. The conversation and question would have to wait for another time as all attention was back on the newly married couple.

The reception line was full of well wishes, hugs, kisses and tears. Happy tears, but tears none the less. Everyone was told about the reception at the hotel just down the street. There was an hour until the reception would actually start, but there were hors d'oeuvres and an open bar to keep the guests entertained while the wedding party took their pictures.

"Want to meet me there, Janelle?" Logan questioned not sure if he should stay with them while they took pictures or go to the reception hall and wait.

"Aren't you going to stay here with me and drive me to the reception?" She asked expecting an affirmative answer from him.

"Sure, honey. I just didn't know if you wanted private time for the pictures." He could not stop smiling when he looked at her.

"Private time doesn't mean you go, Logan.

Private time means *you* stay," she said that with a teasing tone in her voice that let Logan know the woman he loved had a temptress hiding under that reserved exterior.

Hell, he thought to himself, *all she has to do is be here and I am tempted.* Logan leaned over, moved her hair and gently kissed the side of her neck just below her ear.

Janelle shivered and wished it was she and Logan heading out for two weeks in Maui. She looked up at him thinking it was the perfect time for a real kiss.

"Bride's family," the photographer shouted. He was in full swing. Janelle smiled and started to walk toward the front of the church. Logan took her arm and escorted her. He had heard the warning about her tripping and knew that her time out of her neck brace had been given with much reservation on the part of her doctor.

Everyone who was part of the wedding, related to the bride and groom or ever wanted to be related to the bride and groom had their photographs taken. When they could think of no more photograph options at the church, they decided to leave, catch the photographs at the limo, and then move to the reception where there would be many more photos of dancing, toasting, kissing, hugging, eating and merriment in general. It was a perfect day.

As Janelle went to get into Logan's truck she remembered she needed to put her neck brace on before she rode. "Logan," she said softly. She hated this moment. In her mind it was as if it didn't exist if she didn't mention it. "Will you help me?" She showed him the brace and gave him a mock pout. "Doctor's orders. I am like Cinderella and her glass slipper only I had a ceremony and pictures, not until midnight before "bang" back into a pumpkin."

"Well, I did search for you and you are beautiful, you have that part right," he retorted smiling as he took the brace and gently, very gently, placed it back on and fastened the buckles in the back.

He looked at her and smiled. She felt stupid and clumsy standing there. "Doesn't exactly go with the dress does it?" She asked nervously knowing he also wished she wasn't wearing the brace.

"Actually," he paused for a moment and then began again. "I was thinking how much I love your brace for keeping that beautiful head attached to your beautiful shoulders." He reached out his hand to help her into the truck. The reception awaited.

Everyone clapped and cheered as the wedding party began to enter the reception hall. Music played and little confetti pieces that said "Sarah & Mitch" fell in all different colors. As the D.J. announced the Bride and Groom everyone stood and balloons fell as they walked in. It was a fun time and Mitch and Sarah stood for pictures and more well wishes. Janelle noticed that on the gift table was a money tree that had every small branch covered I dollar bills tied to them. What a wonderful addition to the table full of gifts.

The buffet line was opened and after the wedding party and family filled their plates, everyone else followed. Finally Daniel announced to everyone it was time to toast the happy couple and the caterers filled everyone's champagne glasses with champagne or sparkling cider.

The toasting invitation was made. Janelle wanted to toast the couple first and she stood.

"Sarah, Mitch, this has been a perfect day. The two of you define what love should be. You give an example to those around you of selflessness and caring. I am proud to know you both. Sarah, I want you to be the happiest wife in the world and I want for you to be as loved as a woman ever has been, you have a good start already. Mitch, I want you to be respected and loved and I want people to know how much you are loved by Sarah by her actions. May you always be as content and trusting of each other as you are right this moment. I love you both and wish you the happiest and most devoted of lives together."

Janelle leaned over and kissed Sarah's upturned cheek. Mitch took her hand and squeezed it.

Mitch's brother Daniel tapped on his champagne glass to call for other toasts.

Mr. Beckett stood and toasted the couple. "May the sun always shine on your face. Remember that a marriage is the toughest job you will ever love. Oh wait, maybe that was the Marines." Everyone laughed. "In any event you two, you both come from long lines of love. Sarah I have loved your mother every moment since before I ever decided to ask her to marry me. Now, there have been moments we haven't liked each other much, but the commitment was never in question. I wish that for you. Mitch, your parents sit here with you. That tells me what a long line of love you come from. They look at each other and then gaze at the world with one purpose. I wish that for you both also. I also wish that in due time, you will give me grandchildren while I am still able to enjoy them. Salud!" He was beaming.

Sarah's eyes popped open and she looked nervously at Mitch. He kissed her as if to say 'it was a coincidence' and then thanked Mr. Beckett.

Mitch's brother David stood "May all your children be born naked!" Again laughter.

The first dance, dollar dance and father and daughter dance were all photographed for posterity. Laughter, stories of other weddings, pictures, dancing, and children's giggling and games filled the room. It lasted well into the night.

Janelle still grew tired rather easily and was still having issues with severe headaches. She was getting a doozy and decided to leave before it turned into a migraine. She hugged her sister, parents and Mitch and told them she would come to Mom and Dad's tomorrow to watch them open their gifts. Logan offered to drive her home. Sarah just smiled and for a brief moment wondered if Janelle was as "well" physically as she needed to be for an evening alone with Logan. She smiled after the two of them as they walked for the door. She so wanted Janelle to be happy.

Logan and Janelle left the reception. When she got in the truck she closed her eyes in an effort to will the neck and head pain away.

"Anything I can do?" He asked very quietly.

"No. Unfortunately this is a residual effect of almost having your head fall off," she snapped, but Logan knew it was just the pain talking. "I am sorry, Logan. Headaches were never something I tolerated well and these turn into migraines and I hurt to the small of my back by the time they are done."

"Well, let's get you home and see what we can do." He shut off the radio so there would be no noise and drove her home in silence.

Brandy was thrilled to see them when they came into the kitchen. Logan took her out to the grass area and Janelle went and changed into her pajamas. She didn't have it in her to dress her best, even for Logan at that moment.

"Ah, I see you slipped into something more comfortable, Caramia," he drawled as he approached her standing at the sink.

She laughed and smiled at him. "Sorry I am such a party pooper. This is going to sound real forward, and I don't mean for it to, but I am going to lie down in my bedroom with the lights off, want to join me and talk to me for a while?"

Logan feigned shock and placed his hand over his nose and mouth. "As I live and breathe Janelle Beckett what would your father say?"

The two walked to Janelle's room. She stacked a bunch of pillows on her side of the bed and reclined against them. "I left you a couple Logan," she stated as if he was accusing her with his eyes. They were very much at ease and playful together.

Logan reclined beside her and arranged the pillows to where she was almost lying on his shoulder. He was perfectly content.

"Logan. Tell me what happened with Kelly and Patrick. And more about Jake." She was lying with her eyes closed.

"Wow, where to begin..." his voice faded off.

"Once upon a time," Janelle giggled as she spoke realizing this would be a tough story for him to tell and hoping to take the edge off slightly.

"Once upon a time, Janelle! My brother flew to Oklahoma to look at some steers for Dad and me." The tale continued and he talked about his family until he realized Janelle was asleep.

Logan quietly and carefully got off the bed and went to take Brandy outside. When he came back into Janelle's house, Logan decided it best he sleep on the couch. She hadn't told him to leave, and he wasn't expecting to be in Texas overnight again, so he didn't keep his hotel room. The couch it would be. Logan hoped Janelle felt better in the morning.

CHAPTER FORTY-FOUR

Janelle's headache was gone when she woke the next morning. She and Logan had a late breakfast together and Janelle showed him pictures from her childhood. They talked of their lives and learned more about each other than they had been able to ever discuss before. Soon it was time to go to the Beckett's house to meet Mitch and Sarah to open their presents.

"Janelle," Logan almost sounded apologetic. "I'm going to have to leave this evening to drive home. We are just finishing a cattle round up, I have steer deliveries being made this week and I have to be there. I feel like we've been apart a long time and I hate to leave."

"Hmm." Janelle's only response was a sound as she realized Logan had just presented her with a problem she intended to solve.

Logan watched her and could see the wheels spinning behind her beautiful eyes. "Hmmm?"

"Well, we will see what we have to do Logan so we can still see each other. For now, let's go see what amazing things my sister and Mitch got two of that I can take home one of." Her eyes sparkled. She was so very glad to be in her own skin at that very moment.

The afternoon was delightful. Mitch and Sarah certainly received everything they could ever have needed or wanted and then some. They also received almost one thousand dollars in cash that would come in very handy for their honeymoon expenses. Goodbyes were said as the happy couple were leaving first thing in the morning for their two week honeymoon in Maui.

Logan and Janelle were leaving that evening so Logan could get on the road. As they approached the truck, Janelle made her decision.

"Mom, Dad, Sarah, Mitch, and you too Logan. I have made a decision and since you are all standing here I want to tell you all at the same time."

Everyone looked at her with wide, quizzical eyes.

"As you know, my lease has been up for months now and my landlord is just being a doll in letting me stay without a new one because of the accident and all. In any event, I am giving my notice to move out." There, that part was over. She paused for reaction.

"Oh honey," her mother said and then asked, "have you found a new place?"

"No, but I am going to start looking for one tomorrow," Janelle continued, but still did not make it to the big reveal of this conversation. For a fleeting moment Janelle thought she should have talked to Logan privately first, but it was too late now. He was leaving and she needed to tell him.

"I can drive you around tomorrow, Jani," Mr. Beckett offered since he knew Sarah and Logan would be gone.

"No Dad, thank you, I love you, but I am going to have

Logan help me look." Eventually someone had to figure this out she thought as she continued toying with them.

"Janelle, I told you I have to leave tonight." He would have stayed, but he was expected back and with his dad gone, the buck stopped with him.

"And leave you shall," she announced as if the conversation was officially concluded. Janelle was excited and rather pleased with herself for making the decision so she just stood their smiling.

He tilted his head much in the fashion a dog would when you ask them if they want to go for a walk.

Sarah laughed. "You are completely confusing everyone now baby sister. I know you have something up your sleeve so spill it."

"Yeah, what gives, Janelle?" Logan asked. A thought began forming deep in his heart and he had an ever hopeful flare up as it did.

"You're leaving tonight and I'm going with you. I want to go to Flagstaff and find an apartment. I will come back here after that and pack my stuff. I had planned on being in Arizona to go to school. I see no reason my plan can't start. Today." She had her arms crossed in front of her. The stance and determination in her eyes were well known to her family.

"Oh." Her father wasn't surprised. "Well, then that settles that doesn't it." He hugged her and pointed at Logan. "Don't hurt my little girl, Logan, Logan - what is your last name anyway?"

"Logan. My given name is Shannon David Logan. My dad was always Shannon and when I was little my Mom called me "Shane" until one day a babysitter started calling me Little Logan. Logan sort of stuck and I have been just Logan ever since."

"Take care of my daughter while she is with you Shannon David Logan." Mr. Beckett shook Logan's hand.

Sarah just stared at the two of them. She was glad Logan had been persistent. She felt confident that he was telling Janelle the truth and they would be happy.

"I will see you all in a few weeks. You better show me your honeymoon pictures when you get back, you two!"

Goodbyes were said again and Logan helped Janelle into the truck. Janelle knew she wouldn't need to pack much to be gone for a couple weeks. Logan just smiled ear to ear and looked like a Cheshire cat. This trip had certainly turned out better than expected.

CHAPTER FORTY-FIVE

"This is perfect," Janelle announced to the realtor who showed her the little apartment available for rent not too far from Shannon's Luck. It sat on the property of a very large ranch. "How is it this place is actually for rent?"

"The eldest son lived here for a while. He has moved out of state and the family decided to rent it if the right person came along. Logan told them you were the perfect person." They kept walking around. The place was small and Janelle would have to store a lot of her belongings, but that was fine with her. This place was perfect. They signed the contract and Janelle wrote a check for the deposit and first month's rent. She had a one year lease and the owners had agreed to make it very flexible. Janelle could extend it or shorten it as was needed.

Logan and Janelle planned the trip to Abilene to retrieve Janelle's belongings. They intended to stay there for a week and pack her things into his 18 foot cattle trailer. Sarah and Mitch would be back and dinner would be in order to see all the beautiful honeymoon pictures.

Finally it was time to turn in her keys to her rental

DEBBIE ISBELL

house and actually move to Arizona. Janelle was excited and a little sad. She promised her parents she would come home one weekend a month, or they could come to her. After hugs and tears, they left.

. . . .

It took her about two weeks, but Janelle finally unpacked her last box. She told Logan she would cook him dinner at her place because he had been such a help to her in everything that she ever needed done. Brandy had decided to be Janelle's dog. The rental apartment/cabin had a small fenced yard approximately three hundred feet in all directions. It was perfect for her and Janelle was home much more than Logan was.

Janelle had registered for site based classes at the University in Flagstaff and added on a couple of internet classes she would begin taking in about three weeks. She was finally doing it. It wasn't the law school, but that would also come in due time.

The doorbell rang and it was Logan. "Wow you're early," Janelle said as she opened the door. "Oh man do you smell good." She melted against his chest as she spoke. "Soap, beer and I don't know what." She inhaled deeply and sighed.

Logan felt his body respond to her being that close to him. It had been near impossible to be a gentleman with her at all times. God knew he wanted her. He would never push. He was so afraid Janelle would literally break in his arms that he always touched her like she was a china doll. "Easy there, Jani. I am only flesh and blood here." His eyes were dark when she looked up at him.

"You want me don't you?" She asked in the deep matter of fact voice of a woman who already knew the answer. She felt empowered by the way Logan looked at her. She decided to play just a little.

Logan caught on to this immediately. "No, not really, I want dinner." He set her gently out of his arms and walked past her and into the living room. Logan swatted her behind as he walked away.

Janelle gasped and then laughed. She loved him and was feeling pretty pleased with herself for enrolling in school, getting her packing undone and for finally being able to have Logan over with no work to be done. She wasn't ready to back down from the game yet.

Janelle walked past Logan and sat on the couch. He followed. She stood briefly to fold both legs underneath her as she leaned her arm across the back of the couch. With her free hand she unbuttoned five of six buttons until her cleavage and pink bra showed through. In her best Mae West voice she drawled at Logan as she twisted her hair onto her head with one hand. "See anything you like cowboy?"

Logan saw plenty that he liked. Logan saw plenty he loved. Enough was enough, damn it. Logan leaned in and kissed Janelle and ran his hand gently along the nape of her neck and up into her gathered hair. Janelle gasped slightly has Logan's hand tightened gently in her hair. That was all it took to snap Logan back to reality.

Logan instantly broke the kiss and dropped his hand from her hair. *Damn it Logan,* he scolded himself silently, *you could snap her neck!*

"Janelle, I am so sorry. Please tell me I didn't hurt you," he pleaded. He would never forgive himself if he did anything to hurt her.

"No, no, Logan. Nothing happened. Really. Come back here with that mouth," she said and tried to wiggle back into the embrace he had her in.

"Janelle. No, we can't do this. I don't know. I mean, dammit. Did you ask your doctor if you can do this?" He was so concerned and he was so male. He was dying here trying to keep himself in check. He had no choice and would not chance hurting her. Logan reminded himself that he was not sixteen and told himself to calm right the hell down.

Janelle pouted and sat back. She was mad. She didn't want him to stop kissing her. She would certainly be asking the doctor about her physical health. She also realized they really hadn't discussed anything about how this relationship was going to progress.

"Button your shirt and let's have dinner, Janelle. I have to get off this couch before we do something we might regret." He stood and reached for her hand to help her stand.

"Dinner it is," Janelle said, trying not to sound hurt, but it didn't work. She was embarrassed and stood not accepting Logan's outstretched hand. She started to walk past Logan to the kitchen, but he gently stopped her by taking hold of her hand.

"Don't you think for one remote second that I don't want to take you into that bedroom and make love to you for hours, Janelle. I just don't want to take any chances with your health. It's going to kill me, but I will wait until the time is right. Right all the way around. Capiche?" He let her arm go without waiting for an answer.

Janelle turned and hugged him, regretting feeling like such a child. She pressed her face into his chest and kissed his shirt. "Capiche," she answered smiling up at Logan with tears starting to form in her eyes.

"It's okay, Janelle. It is. We'll figure this all out," Logan said smiling at her. She smiled back, nodded and walked into the kitchen so they could eat.

CHAPTER FORTY-SIX

The weeks had flown by, Janelle was so pleased that she had finished two of the required six week classes on line. She had loved going to visit her family and Sarah's belly was getting so big. It made Janelle want a baby. Sarah knew what she was having, but they were keeping it to themselves so everyone would be surprised.

Jake had come to stay with Logan for a few weeks and Janelle had fallen in love with that little boy. She saw how easy it was for Logan to be attached to Jake and his mom. The time had come for Jake to go home and Janelle was truly going to miss him until he returned at summer time.

***

Logan told Janelle that he had to take a trip into Wickenburg for cows. He asked if Janelle wanted to go with him. She decided to pass as she had a lot of work to get done on her new class assignments. She wanted to be ahead so she would have time to spend with Sarah when the baby came. Logan promised that when he returned he would take her for a long drive and introduce her to squirrel hunting, the most fun anyone could have on a drive. It was getting cooler now and the hunting season had opened. Logan seemed genuinely pleased that the time had come. He told Janelle he was going to be gone four days. While he was gone Janelle would call and schedule to see Dr. Curtis, next month was six months since he released her from his care. It was hard for her to fathom that it was nine months since the accident.

Everything would be perfect if he told her she was healthy and able to go back to being a woman, but another month. It would be a long one.

CHAPTER FORTY-SEVEN

Logan had been gone four days. There was a knock at Janelle's door. It was only ten in the morning. Janelle expected Logan later in the day, but knew it would be him, home early. She smiled and went to answer the door.

It wasn't Logan. There stood a very pretty, but hard looking young Hispanic woman.

"Are you Janelle?" She asked.

"I am, but I apologize, I don't know your name," Janelle responded still smiling. Everyone had been so kind to her since she had arrived and she was happy to meet a new neighbor.

"I'm Rachel. I am surprised you don't know who I am. Can I talk to you about Logan, please?" She was sounding sweet, but was pissed and had every intention of putting this little crippled woman in her place. Rachel knew who Janelle was. She had seen her reaction the day she left Shannon's Luck in tears and she knew the problem. Now Kelly was gone Rachel expected Logan to turn to her. He was the brother she had really wanted anyway.

"Sure, please do." Janelle had heard some mean things

said about Rachel, and knew the story Logan had told her, but Rachel seemed polite and friendly.

Janelle walked to the kitchen and sat at the breakfast nook with Rachel.

"Well," Rachel began, "you probably heard some things about me, but they probably aren't entirely true or fair."

Janelle smiled slightly at the awkward comment and continued listening.

"You see, several, several years ago Logan and I were sort of an item. He was going to marry me. Then his brother, Patrick, got mixed up with that Kelly girl. You probably know her and her kid. Anyway, Logan's interest waned and he spent less and less time with me. They got married, Patrick and Kelly, and then had a kid. By then Logan had dropped me out of his life with no explanation. It was a very painful time for me. You see, I was pregnant with Logan's child. I was crazy with the hurt and I unfortunately turned to drinking and drugs to dull the pain. I lost the baby. I wanted Logan to care, but he didn't. One day I went to talk to Logan and Patrick was there. He had been fighting with Kelly because she was so uptight and never let him do anything he wanted to. Well, I mean, see, Patrick did drugs too. Did they tell you that?" Rachel asked.

"I was told about Patrick, Rachel. I am terribly sorry about your baby. I didn't know about the loss." Janelle was sincerely sorry, but was surprised that Logan had never told her this part of his life.

"Yeah, well, not much can be done about that now. Anyway, Patrick died. You know that too I'm sure. I was hopeful that Logan would come back to me, but he became so possessive of Kelly and her kid. It seemed as if they were his family. There was still no room for me and I had waited for him so patiently. So you see, now Kelly is gone and - well, has Logan made any promises to you? Are you engaged or anything?" Rachel just spit that last part out as if it was a regular everyday question.

Janelle was caught off guard by the question and the turn of the conversation. She was taken aback by the callousness with which Rachel had blurted out about Patrick's death and shocked by the revelation she had carried Logan's child. Janelle had no time to process anything she was being told and knew she had to respond.

"Wow, Rachel. I wasn't expecting that question. I mean, Logan and I have been seeing each other, but we aren't engaged or anything." Janelle didn't feel she could claim a tie to Logan by any promises as none had been made.

"Oh, well then if I wanted to see him, you wouldn't mind?" Emotionless voices were speaking between the two women as if it were an exchange of unwanted hand-me-downs and not a man.

"I guess Logan is a grown man, Rachel. He can do what he wants. I just want him to be happy." Janelle was hurt, but owed Logan honesty to his friends. Janelle did her best not to let the anger she was feeling toward Rachel seep into her voice. Honestly, Janelle realized, the questions was fairly asked. Although Janelle wanted Logan's happiness to be with her, not another woman, she had no intention of telling that to Rachel.

"Good, I intend to pursue him. Janelle, if you really care about him, you won't try to stop me. See, don't get your feelings hurt, but Logan is a very vibrant man who loves life. He loves to work hard and play hard. He loves to hunt, boat and fish. You would hold him back. I know about your accident and that you are, well, crippled now.

Logan will cling to you like he clung to Kelly, because you need him. He will tire of you though. He's never been as happy as he was with me and, well to be honest, being needy isn't very attractive." She shrugged and half smiled at Janelle. Rachel was spiteful in her conversation with Janelle. She intended to win.

"Rachel, Logan is a grown man. He will do whatever he wants to do. You, nor I can change that," Janelle's voice was curt and just a little louder than it needed to be. Janelle wanted this woman out of her house.

"Well. If you care about him, give him a week with me. He will remember how much he cares about me if you will butt out of his life for a while you know." Rachel was getting angry and lost the fake smile and kindness she had started the conversation with.

"I think you should go. If you want to have a discussion about Logan's life, speak to him. He is not a car we can agree to let one or the other of us drive. Logan is a grown man, he is the one who will decide what do to with his life. It seems to me that he finished with you years ago Rachel. Perhaps Logan has already made his decision." Janelle was already walking toward the door as she spoke. "Please leave Rachel. I don't want you in my house."

Rachel smiled, but it was more of a sneer. She walked slowly to the door, hesitated as she rudely stared at Janelle. Rachel looked Janelle up and down as if weighing the completion. She shook her head and then turned and left the house confident Janelle would be concerned just enough that Rachel was right. That concern would make Janelle give Rachel and Logan the space Rachel knew they needed whether Janelle wanted to or not. This would give Rachel a chance. She didn't care that she was lying to Janelle about almost everything she had said. All was fair in love and war. To Rachel, this was war.

***

It was only an hour later when Logan knocked on the door. Janelle knew she shouldn't believe what Rachel had said about Logan, but the story tugged at her emotions. Janelle was feeling very insecure about herself. Janelle opened the door. Logan smiled and opened his arms to hug her. Janelle felt herself tense up as Logan wrapped his arms around her.

"Hey, Janelle, what's wrong?" Logan had waited all day to see her and didn't expect that reaction from her. "Are you feeling alright? Is everything okay?" He loosened his arms and Janelle willingly stepped back and out of his embrace.

"Come in," Janelle said walking away from the door and toward the couch to sit down. "Rachel came to see me. Seems she wants you Logan and decided to tell me to butt-out, so to speak. Did you date her, Logan? Am I stepping on her toes?" Janelle had to be sure.

Logan cursed under his breath. God he hated that woman. "Absolutely not, Janelle. I was the only man our age that didn't have her. I was never interested." Logan was angry and his voice betrayed that fact.

"She told me that my handicap would stop you from doing what you want in life. That made me wonder. I mean, you deserve to just go where you want and react when you want to. You won't even make love to me because of this damned neck issue." Janelle stood and walked toward the kitchen. She was nervous and couldn't handle seeing the look in Logan's eyes which would tell her more than his words ever could. Janelle took a deep breath and willed herself not to cry.

"I won't make love to you? Is that the deciding factor on

whether or not I want you, Janelle?" Logan stepped forward and took her in his arms and kissed her. Any doubt that she may have had was going to be gone when he was finished with this kiss. That, and whatever came after. She started to protest, but didn't really want to so she gave in to Logan's kiss. He kissed her long and hard and then gently. Logan broke their embrace and reached down to grab her hand. He started walking toward the bedroom. When his hand felt the resistance from Janelle not walking, he tugged on her hand, and kept walking to the bedroom. Once inside, he stopped, turned and kissed her again.

He stepped back, took her face gently in his hands and spoke softly. "I do want you Janelle. I know we have to be aware of your neck, but that certainly doesn't make me not want you." Logan stared into her eyes. His voice was deep and hungry. "Of course I want you, Janelle," he whispered as he lowered his mouth and kissed her again.

Logan ran his hands under her shirt and rubbed her back. Then he reached around and unbuttoned her blouse. He backed her up to the bed and lowered her as he kissed her chin and the portion of her neck that was showing above the brace. He would not ignore her body, the brace was a part of her at this point in time. He pulled her blouse off and kissed the hollow between her breasts. He had a moment of doubt at she tensed.

"Tell me stop, Janelle. If you want me to stop, you need to tell me now," he was talking into her skin, never lifting his head.

Janelle could feel how much he wanted her. The tensing was from her own desire. "Don't stop Logan. Please. Don't stop." She ran her hands across his shoulders and loved the feel of his chiseled muscles under her hands. She reached to unbutton his shirt. Logan sat up and took his shirt off.

The two slowly, lovingly explored each other's bodies. They loved gently and they loved passionately. Finally Logan could wait no longer.

"Janelle," he whispered and her name sounded more like a prayer and the thick huskiness of his voice said it all. No other words were necessary. He was asking for permission, he was asking if she was ready. He was begging to take her.

Janelle said nothing. She smiled and pulled Logan's head down. She kissed him again deeply.

Logan was gentle, even when Janelle's body was begging for something more. He loved her and she returned his actions until they were both lying spent on the bed. Logan was lying with his head on Janelle's stomach trying to regain his breath and remember when he had ever felt as complete as he did at that very moment.

"You are perfect for me Janelle. Perfect for me." He kissed her stomach and she tangled her fingers in his hair. "I want no other woman. Ever."

"Oh Logan." Janelle felt a tear slide down her cheek.

The two fell asleep and slept for a couple of hours. Janelle woke before Logan who had rolled onto his side and was sleeping soundly facing away from her. Somehow Brandy had made it onto the bed and was sleeping curled at Logan's knees.

Janelle smiled at the sight of the two of them. She disregarded the thought that Brandy should not learn to sleep on the bed. She had grown so much already and was obviously going to be a rather big dog.

Janelle got up and dressed. Tonight she wanted to go out. She felt as if her life had gained new meaning and she certainly felt like celebrating. All thoughts of Rachel were gone. She simply did not matter. She did not matter to Logan and she did not matter to Janelle.

***

Today was the promised road trip. Logan was going to squirrel hunt and Janelle was going to enjoy the scenery. She was just happy to spend the day with Logan. They finally made it to the right spot, or so Logan told her.

"Look for squirrels or we will have no dinner tonight." He sounded like a little boy. She loved the freedom she heard in his voice.

"And exactly how does one hunt squirrels, Logan? You aren't going to shoot them from the truck are you?" She asked laughing.

"Just you watch, honey. Just you watch." He was smiling and concentrating very hard out the window.

Without warning Logan pulled over, put the truck in park, and was yelling "squirrel" as he threw open his door, grabbed his gun and took off running after a little grey squirrel with a large white and grey tail. Logan ran and the squirrel immediately ran too. It ran past one or two trees and then ran straight up the tallest of the three Ponderosa Pines that were in the small stand of trees.

Janelle was laughing to herself and enjoying watching Logan "hunt." She watched him walk around and around the tree. Soon he sighted the gun toward the top of the tree and pulled the trigger. Janelle watched the squirrel fall to the ground.

She got out of the truck and walked over toward him. Brandy ran over and was barking at the squirrel.

"That, my dear, is how one hunt's squirrels." He bowed gallantly.

"Wow. You're a great shot, Logan. Guess I won't have to starve in the winter after all. So, we can eat these right?" Janelle was admiring Logan's shot precision.

"Four more and we have dinner." He picked up the squirrel and walked toward the truck.

The two enjoyed the day and it was getting late into the afternoon. Logan had one squirrel left to find.

"Want to walk some Janelle? I can bag out while we walk." He may have been talking to her, but his eyes were darting around the forest watching for movement.

"Sure. Logan." She reached for his free hand.

The two walked along what was once a forest road and was now overgrown and closed off to motor vehicles. Logan told her stories of all the times he had hunted as a child with his dad, or with Patrick. He showed her a favorite spot where he would sit and watch for wildlife. They agreed to sit and see what they could find. Brandy fell asleep at Janelle's feet. Logan and Janelle had been sitting for about thirty minutes, in complete silence, when three cow elk came up the ravine. Janelle had an intake of breath and immediately quieted herself. Logan smiled. He knew the awe she was feeling if this was the first time she had ever seen these huge animals. The elk were in no hurry and fortunately Brandy stayed asleep. A large six point bull elk walked up behind the small herd. Janelle sat in complete amazement. She thought to herself this was the most perfect moment. Something, unknown to Janelle or Logan, caught the elk's attention. The bull raised his massive head and all the elk froze. Soon he turned tail and ran, the cows were mere steps behind him.

Janelle jumped to her feet to see if she could still see

SHANNON'S LUCK

them. "Oh Logan! That was so awesome. I have never seen elk before. Oh wow. No wonder you love it here. They scared the bejeezus out of me when they first approached. They are huge!" She was elated and the happiness in her voice was contagious.

"Man woman, look at you. I love your enthusiasm. I will find you any animal you want to see if you would just smile like that for me again." She took his breath away. She caused other reactions too standing there, but Logan chose to ignore them and not act like that rutting bull that just ran off down the ravine, harem in tow.

The rest of the day was equally as enjoyable. Logan got his limit of squirrels and the two went home so Janelle could learn all about cooking them.

   ***

The phone rang early the next morning. As Janelle reached for the phone she realized it was still dark outside. Logan groaned at her side. She didn't want to wake him so she spoke quietly.

"Hello," she whispered quietly.

"Got company?" Came the exuberant voice of her sister on the other end of the line.

"Yes." Janelle was smiling. Sarah knew that though.

"Well, I wondered what you are doing today." Sarah was toying.

Janelle whispered. "Sarah it isn't even 5:00 a.m. here. I haven't even decided if I am going to get out of bed today, let alone what I am going to do."

"Well, if you don't have any plans, how about coming home?" Sarah waited.

"I am home, Sis." Janelle's eyes were sleepy and closing as she whispered to her sister on the phone.

"Well, I thought you might like to come to the hospital and meet your new niece." Sarah knew that statement was going to wake her up.

"Oh my goodness!" Janelle was no longer quiet. She jumped up and sat on the edge of the bed. Logan flew awake at the sound of her shouts. He looked at her concerned. She was smiling, this must be good news. He let himself fall back in bed as if he had been shot and just listened to her talk.

"Sarah! Did you have the baby? How are you? Why didn't you call me earlier? Are you alright? How is the baby? Where is Mitch? Are Mom and Dad there? Oh my goodness, I'm an aunt!" Janelle's face was streaming with happy tears.

Logan sat up and wrapped an arm around her shoulders. She laid her head on his chest and continued talking.

Sarah was laughing on the other end of the phone. "Janelle, it happened rather fast. I had indigestion and asked Mitch if we could go get a soda. We were just going to drive through a fast food place. Right before we got there my water broke, all over the front seat of the car. So, needless to say, it was off to the hospital for the three of us. She was born about an hour ago. You are my first phone call." Sarah was beaming as she spoke.

"Well, you said niece. Tell me all about her. Oh I can't wait to be there. I am leaving today! I promise you I will be there today." Janelle could not remember being happier.

"She is perfect. Ten fingers, ten toes. Two of everything she is supposed to have two of. Her hair is auburn like mine and she has a ton of it. She is 7lbs. 6 ounces. Oh Janelle. She is so perfect. I can't imagine her being mine.

What a perfect gift of love she demonstrates. I named her Zoe. Zoe Elaine. After Mom." Sarah sounded like a truly blessed woman.

The two talked and Janelle finally hung up and, while still holding Janelle against his chest, Logan said "I want to marry you and have a baby Janelle."

"Get dressed Logan you have to take me to the airport." She wasn't about to respond because she was caught up in emotion at this moment and would have said yes to anything. She wanted Logan, wanted to be his wife and wanted to have his children. She wanted him to mean it and not have to ask in an emotional outcry.

Arrangements were made to move up Janelle's ticket scheduled for the following weekend. It only cost a little extra. Logan couldn't go, but told her he would join her at the end of the week.

The two kissed goodbye at the airport and Janelle felt like she was leaving part of her behind when the plane took off.

***

Mitch picked Janelle up from the airport. He was elated and talking non-stop about what a trooper Sarah had been, no pain killers, no epidural, there wasn't time and she didn't scream or hit him or anything. He went on and on about how beautiful his daughter was.

"Wow, Janelle. Did you hear that? My 'daughter' who would have ever thought I would have the most beautiful and perfect wife God ever gave a man and now I have the most beautiful and perfect daughter to go along with her. I can't wait for you to meet her. She is just perfect." Mitch was beaming.

Janelle had a tear running down her cheek. She was so happy for Sarah and Mitch. They were so perfect for each other. She was glad she had purchased gifts ahead of time for a nephew and a niece, so she had the perfect pink lacy little outfit for Zoe and a necklace that said "Mom" for Sarah.

"I am so happy for the two of you. You both deserve all the happiness God wants to shed on you. I can't wait to hug my sister. Imagine Sarah a mother. That just overwhelms me. She will be so perfect." Janelle was almost jumping out of her skin with happiness.

They arrived at the hospital and it was all the two of them could do to walk to the elevator and then from the elevator to Sarah's room. Sarah was holding Zoe when they walked in.

"Janelle!" Sarah was thrilled to see her sister.

There were instant happy tears. "Look at her Janelle. Isn't she the most beautiful baby you have ever seen?"

Janelle sat on Sarah's bed and took Zoe from her. Janelle rested the baby on her legs so she could get a good look at her sweet face. Even the soft brace made it difficult for Janelle to see the baby if she cradled her against her chest. She was so tiny. Janelle was overwhelmed by how helpless a tiny newborn was. "Wow, Sarah. I can't imagine being responsible for every part of someone's life. It is certainly a large responsibility, but just look at your reward!"

"I know. I know. I was going to call you when I went into labor. That was the plan anyway. It happened so fast." Sarah began the age old ritual of telling every moment by moment happening with the birth of her first child. She would retell this story whenever she attended a baby shower, whenever someone told about someone's child birth dilemma, although she would tell of the great pain, it was already forgotten and her heart knew she would gladly do it again for her child.

"She is just perfect, Sarah. You too Mitch, great job on the baby making with my sister." Janelle winked at him and he put his arm around her as she sat cooing at Zoe and touching her little hand and kissing her tiny cheek. Everything was once again right with the world.

"So, Janelle," Mitch began in a voice that spoke with pure contentment and playfulness too. "When are you going to marry that big strong rancher who so obviously adores you and give Zoe here a cousin?"

"Yeah Janelle. I would love to go to a wedding in Arizona and then come see my niece or nephew." Sarah reached out to Janelle's arm and rubbed it lovingly.

"Whoa, whoa, you two. I have to get used to being an aunt, I don't have time to be a mom too. Plus, I have schooling I want to complete, Logan hasn't asked me to marry him, well, yes he has on several occasions, but I don't think he was serious. If he was…" Janelle was still talking when Sarah heard what she wanted to hear and interrupted.

"Wait!" Sarah exclaimed. "Did you just say he has asked you on several occasions? Why aren't you getting married? I know you love him, I can see it in your eyes. I know he loves you, I mean the man traipsed all the way from Flagstaff to Abilene and bought 27 cows and 3 bulls just to have an excuse to hunt you down when your sister, who shall remain nameless because she is talking right now, tried to keep him away from you, because I love you!" Sarah took a breath and smiled waiting for an explanation.

Janelle looked at Mitch who had his eyebrows raised and was looking at her with a look Janelle knew he would be giving Zoe when she was older and she was not really in trouble, but Mitch would have to pretend to disapprove. He crossed his arms as he stared at her for a more desired effect.

"Well Janelle? Is there anything you would like to say to your sister and me?" He was looking at her with mock sternness.

Janelle put the baby up on her shoulder and stood to hug Mitch. "I adore you two. No, Mitch." She looked at her sister. "No, Sarah. I have nothing to tell you. If I do have anything to tell you I will. Deal?"

Mitch and Sarah nodded and simultaneously said "Deal."

***

Sarah and Zoe had been home four days when Logan finally arrived in town. Janelle and Mitch went to the airport to pick him up and when they returned to the house the Becketts were there adoring their first grandchild.

"Daddy." Janelle hugged her father. God she missed her parents while she was in Arizona. She had not seen them since she got to town as her father had been sick and so they stayed away from the baby. This was the first time they saw her.

"Hi Baby," Mr. Beckett said to Janelle holding his precious daughter to him. "You are more beautiful than ever. That cool air must agree with you. You have more color in your cheeks than I have seen in years." He smiled at her. "Zoe is the spitting image of the two of you when you were born. Except her nose is Mitch. She is certainly a precious gift in our lives that one is."

Janelle hugged and kissed her mother. Her mother took her face in both her hands and stared into her eyes as if that simple act would answer any questions that could come to mind. Her mother smiled a knowing smile and slowly nodded. Janelle gave her mother an inquisitive cock of her head.

"What Mom?" She asked.

"In due time my dear. In due time." She walked over to Logan and hugged him. Logan looked over Mrs. Beckett's head to Janelle. Janelle rolled her eyes thinking her mother was feeling rather melodramatic. It must be the baby.

Logan and Mitch were talking about the baby and the ranch and the Becketts were again adoring Zoe. Sarah sat and soaked up the love in her home. Janelle went to get Logan's small suitcase and move it into Sarah and Mitch's guest room.

"Oh no, Janelle," her mother exclaimed. "Do not lift that yourself."

"Momma I am fine. Really. The doctor said lifting things will not hurt my neck. That is why I have this brace, to make sure nothing snaps. I am fine. Enjoy Zoe." Janelle continued what she was doing.

"Absolutely not, Janelle Beckett!" Her mother was curt. The tone in her voice was one rarely heard. Everyone immediately stopped and stared wide eyed at Mrs. Beckett.

"Ok Momma. I'm sorry. Logan...," Janelle began, but Logan was already three steps toward her and turning to apologize to Mrs. Beckett.

"I am sorry. I should have moved the case myself." He didn't understand why she was so forceful about this. Everyone knew that Janelle was capable of doing things for herself now and that she knew her limitations. He decided not to worry about it and walked back to the guest bedroom.

Logan sat the suitcase on a chair by the window. When he turned to leave Mrs. Beckett was standing there.

"Ho. You startled me, Mrs. Beckett." Logan smiled and walked toward her.

"Logan do you love my daughter?" She asked pointedly with no smile on her face. "Or are you toying with her until you are bored?"

"Wow, Mrs. Beckett where did that come from? Did I offend you somehow? I am sorry about the suitcase...," he started.

"I don't really give a damn about that suitcase

Shannon. I am asking you if you love my daughter." She was standing in the door way. She was tiny, but did not appear so at that moment.

"I love Janelle very much. She is part of my world. I told her, and I will tell you. I loved her before I ever knew her and when I met her, my love made sense. I want her in my life forever. I have asked her to marry me, but she never answers me." He touched Mrs. Beckett's soft wrinkled cheek and stated very softly. "I love her with my entire being."

"Make her want to marry you then Logan. My daughter is carrying your child." Mrs. Beckett looked him right in the eye. It was not a judgmental stare, but Logan felt as if he had been given a direct order.

"What?" Obviously Logan didn't know.

"I don't think she knows either, Logan. A mother knows these things. Ask her to marry you before she finds out. She will say 'no' for sure then thinking you are only asking because of the baby. She is a stubborn and self-sufficient one that Janelle is. Now Sarah, I knew she was pregnant when she got married. She would rather die than tell her father and me. Janelle though. No. She would announce she was pregnant and tell us all to stuff our opinions. She has spunk. You need to ask her soon. That is, if you mean what you are saying. You have to take her breath away." Mrs. Beckett knew Janelle well and she obviously approved of their being together.

Logan hugged his soon to be mother-in-law and went to find Janelle. His mind was swirling with thoughts on how to take Janelle's breath away so she had no choice and no desire except to say 'yes' to Logan's proposal.

***

The two weeks with her family had been wonderful and Janelle hated leaving them. She hated that Zoe would be growing without Janelle seeing her every day. She was very teary eyed at the thought of going, but the thought of staying and not being a part of Logan's world was even worse.

Logan and Janelle were ready to leave and had to return their rental car to the airport and turn it in. Goodbyes were said and Mrs. Beckett gave Logan a final hug and then turned to Janelle to hug her. While she held her she said something that made no sense to Janelle at the time.

"Baby, sometimes you have to let your life get messy to prove you're really alive. Don't be so stubborn. Listen to your heart." Mrs. Beckett kissed her daughter and smiled nodding at her.

"Ok Momma," Janelle responded laughing nervously at her mother and wondering why she was acting so strange. It was time to go.

***

Janelle and Logan had been home two or three weeks and everything was getting back to a normal routine.

Janelle enrolled in another on line class and it was starting soon. For now she was just relaxing and watching a home improvement show on television. It was late and Logan stayed at his house because he had ranch business and a late meeting with his business advisor. Brandy was asleep on the couch with her head on Janelle's lap. She had turned into a strong beautiful dog. She loved Janelle and never wanted to leave her side.

Janelle was lost in thought when the phone rang. "Hello?" she answered.

"Hi beautiful," Logan said quietly, sounding almost sad.

"Hey, what's wrong?" Janelle was worried instantly. Her eyes felt tearful and she rolled her eyes at how easily he pulled emotions from her. She wondered when she became such a crybaby.

"I just miss you. Do me a favor?" He asked.

"Anything," she responded smiling as she spoke.

"Meet me at Dad's. I want to take you for a ride over the Canyon," he said smiling, but trying not to sound too excited.

"What about your meeting, Logan?"

"It's over. Well, my part is anyway. This is important Janelle. I want you to come with me." He sounded as if this was a life changing moment.

"Ok Logan. Let me put my shoes on and grab a jacket. I'll meet you there in about fifteen minutes." Janelle stood as she spoke and looked around for her shoes.

"I love you, Janelle. You believe that don't you?" His voice was tender and almost melancholy.

"Logan you aren't going to tell me bad news are you? You are scaring me." Janelle wanted him in front of her so she could see his face.

"No bad news baby. Fifteen minutes." He hung up.

***

Logan was waiting when Janelle arrived. He walked up to her and took her hand. "Come on," was all he said as he showed her to his truck.

The two drove to the small airpark located closer to the City. A man in coveralls approached and pointed toward a small plane. "Over here."

"Logan?" She queried seeing the man was pointing to a very small plane.

"No questions. Just watch." He took her hand and led her toward the plane.

They boarded the small plane, took their seats and buckled their seatbelts. Janelle was not at all thrilled about this tiny plan, but Logan seemed so excited.

***

The small plane took off and they flew over the lights of town. The plane circled around and was heading toward a large open meadow. Janelle rested her head on Logan's shoulder as she watched out the window. She was content.

Soon the plane started to fly lower. Logan squirmed in his chair and sat up a little straighter. Janelle looked at him as if he was crazy. He nodded toward the window and smiled at her. She turned to look out the window as Logan kissed her gently on her shoulder and whispered almost too quietly to be sure she even heard him. "You are my life Janelle."

Janelle was trying to process what Logan had said when she saw bright lights outside the window. Janelle could not believe her eyes. As she looked out over the field there was spelled out in lights, probably nine feet high letters that read:

MARRY ME PLEASE JANELLE

She had never had a moment like this. She turned and looked shocked at Logan and then she broke into a huge smile. Tears were running down her face. The pilot circled around and Janelle looked back out the window. The pilot had taken a photograph of the field with a camera attached to the plane and he would make sure they received a copy to remember the moment.

Janelle hugged Logan tightly and said "Oh Logan, you take my breath away. Yes, yes I will marry you Shannon Logan!" The two kissed and pilot smiled to himself and then turned the plane around to fly back to the airpark.

***

Janelle was adamant that she only wanted a small wedding. She would get a simple floor length dress she could wear again in the future for some festive event. Janelle wanted to be married where she and Logan met; at Shannon's Luck. Her family was thrilled when they heard the news and all agreed to drive out for the event. The wedding would come quickly. Janelle did not want to sleep alone at her house one more night than she had to now that she admitted to herself she really did want to be Logan's wife.

***

Today was Janelle's last drive to Phoenix to see Dr. Curtis. She was so excited to be driving herself. Her replacement BMW was sitting out front of the cabin and she expected Dr. Curtis to reduce the amount of time or situations when Janelle would have to wear the soft brace. Perhaps only when she was doing something strenuous or that would jog her around. That is what Janelle hoped. She was excited that she and Logan had planned a one week honeymoon in Southern California. Janelle was excited about going sailing, relaxing and being a tourist. She really didn't want to have to wear the damned brace the whole time she was gone.

She was dressed and had fed Brandy. The dog was not happy that she had to stay home. She was too used to going everywhere Janelle went.

"I will make it up to you with a big bone after dinner tonight, ok, Brandy?" Janelle was holding her head and looking right into her maple brown eyes. She scratched the dog's head and then picked up her purse to leave.

Janelle sat in her BMW and smiled. Finally, she was going to drive herself somewhere. It had been so long she had to be chauffeured around and she had always loved to drive. This new car on the highway would make it even more exciting. She was glad to be leaving early so there wouldn't be much traffic.

Janelle inhaled the new car smell and giggled with excitement to drive her new car. She turned over the key in the ignition and hummed a satisfying sound when the car was purring and waiting to drive off. Janelle adjusted the driver's and passenger side mirror and moved her hand to adjust the rear view mirror. At that moment a sickness washed over her. She felt herself sweating and going into a panic. The accident scene she had been unable to remember ran vividly across her memory. She was clutching the steering wheel with both hands until her fingers were white. Janelle heard the screeching of the car in front of her. She saw the eighteen wheeler come around the corner and collide head on into the vehicle in front of her. She saw the car behind her hit her BMW she heard herself scream. Did she remember herself screaming, or was she actually screaming? She was crying and felt pain all over. She remembered nothing else. Janelle sat trapped in the memory and frozen in place. She was crying and could not let go of the steering wheel or move her eyes from the rearview mirror. She struggled to even catch her breath. It was awful, why did she remember now?

"Someone please help me," she cried out not sure if she was actually saying the words or if they were just screaming over and over in her mind.

Brandy was at the side of her car barking incessantly. She knew something was wrong with her master and she wasn't going to stop until Janelle got out of the car.

Suddenly the door opened and Janelle heard Logan cooing at her.

"Come on, honey. Everything is going to be fine. You are fine. Come on Janelle. Let's get out of the car." He was speaking so quietly that if his head had not been right next to her ear, she would not have heard him.

He gently removed each of her hands from the steering wheel and shut off the engine. He pushed the keys into his pants and crouched beside Janelle still sitting in the car. He rubbed her arm and leg gently and kept talking to her. She was white and shaking and he was worried that she had slipped into shock. He took off his shirt and draped it across her shoulders.

"Janelle," he spoke her name firmly to get her attention, but she did not respond. "Baby, look at me." He was so gentle in begging her to come back from the horrid memory he was so afraid was going to happen.

He sat for a couple more minutes just cooing her name and telling her that everything was going to be fine. He silently cussed himself for not being there when she started to drive off. He should have gone with her even if she drove herself.

Janelle finally turned her face toward him. When she saw him she fell over into his arms and started sobbing. "It was horrible Logan. It was horrible. Why didn't I die in that crash? How did I survive that? Why did I have to remember this now?"

He rubbed her back and kissed her hair. "It's okay, honey. It's ok. We will get you through this and back on the road ok? But not today. Today I am driving you to the doctor. Come on, let's get you out of this car and change your shirt. We have to go then, ok?" He helped her turn her legs and move them out of the car and then he gently pulled Janelle toward him and out of the vehicle.

"I'm sorry Logan. I feel so foolish." She stepped into his arms. She just wanted to be lost there. When he closed his arms around her and rested his head on hers she felt shielded from every bad thing that could ever go on in the world. Slowly, as she stood there, her heartbeat returned to a normal pace. She felt herself relaxing and letting go of that moment when the accident raced back to her. Suddenly she realized that Logan was not supposed to be there that morning. She leaned back, but did not leave his embrace.

"Logan, what were you doing here?" She smiled.

"I should have known you would leave early. I should have come earlier. Actually, I didn't want you to drive yourself, but I knew you needed to do it. I should have been here to at least say 'good bye' and wave you down the road. I was trying not to coddle you by staying away. Then I couldn't stand it anymore. When I approached the cabin I saw Brandy jumping at the car and barking. I saw the car hadn't moved, and neither had you, as I was driving along the road. As I got out of my car, I heard you scream. I'm sorry the memory came back Janelle. I was kind of hoping it never would." He petted her hair as he spoke in a soothing protective manner.

"It had to Logan. Better in the driveway than on the road to Phoenix. Will you drive me, Logan? Can you, I mean?" She was afraid now to be behind the wheel. She had never been afraid to drive.

"I will, but we have to get you driving soon honey. I don't want you 'gun shy' so to speak." He was just glad the moment was over for now.

***

Dr. Curtis was thrilled with Janelle's progress. The MRI showed exactly what he had hoped to see. Her neck bones had completely fused to the implanted bone and to the screws that connected her head and spine. She was a walking miracle. He had performed this surgery two other times since Janelle - once in California and once in Ohio. The young man in California had not been so lucky, he didn't survive the recovery. The man in Ohio was doing well so far, but, just like Janelle had done, was on a long road of recovery.

"Janelle, here is what you have been waiting for someone to tell you," Dr. Curtis said as he smiled at her and removed her neck brace. "You are through with this soft brace. Keep it with you in case you decide to sky dive or something, but you are healed and don't have to wear it any longer."

Janelle jumped off the table and hugged Dr. Curtis. He had saved her life and now he was handing her complete freedom from the accident, from reminders of her injuries that gave her power over the memory that had swept over her earlier that morning.

"Oh, Dr. Curtis, I can't even thank you enough for what

you did!" She was just so pleased to be alive. "I am getting married you know. To Logan. Remember Logan?" She queried.

"Yes I do. Strange how that worked. Him finding you and staying there through all of this. He seems a very good man, Janelle. You two seem so perfect for each other." Dr. Curtis was reaching to shake her hand, knowing he had other patients to see, he felt a little melancholy Janelle was going to be officially out of his life.

"Thank you, Dr. Curtis. For giving me my life back. I know my only other option would have been a slow death if you hadn't been able to perform this surgery."

"It is my way of giving back Janelle. My way of giving back. Be good to yourself and keep loving that man." Dr. Curtis smiled and then turned to leave.

Janelle walked out in the lobby without the soft brace. Logan smiled when he saw her.

"Look at me!" She was beaming. "No brace,

Logan. I am free now!"

He hugged her. "Let's go buy you something low cut and sexy to celebrate what a good boy I have been!" He was laughing.

"What a good boy YOU have been? What about how good a girl I have been?" She teased.

"Well, you have been pretty good. But I really deserve a sexy low cut blouse on my woman." He took her hand and the two left.

***

The wedding had been beautiful. Logan wore a tuxedo with tails and a silver paisley vest. Janelle wore an ivory white t-length gown that dipped slightly lower in the back. The bodice was fitted and had no defined waist, but the skirt flared slightly and had tiny pearl beads along the trim. The dress was strapless and Janelle wore her hair in a partial up do. The back hung down curled into ringlets and she looked beautiful with tiny white pearls and baby's breath tucked into the crown of her hair. She wore a pearl drop that her father had sent her after he heard she was getting married. She wore Logan's mother's ring and Logan wore his father's. It was perfect.

***

As Janelle sat staring in the mirror at herself she could hardly believe that had been twenty years ago. She was looking so forward to the anniversary dinner at Shannon's Luck. Sarah and Mitch would be there. She always missed her parents on occasions such as this when they would have been present. Janelle was excited that Zoe agreed to fly to Arizona from school in Dallas to celebrate Logan and Janelle's twentieth wedding anniversary. She wondered if Sarah ever regretted that she and Mitch had no other children. She could never imagine her life with only one child. Her thoughts continued about her family and how the years had passed. There was a knock at her open bedroom door.

"Mama? Can I come in?" It was Lacey. Her beautiful Lacey who at sixteen was more talented and driven than Janelle had ever been. Janelle remembered how shocked she was to find out she had been two months pregnant when she and Logan married. Janelle had been so busy recovering, she never noticed the telltale signs. When their son had been stillborn Janelle thought she would never recover from the pain. Logan had loved her through it and promised her more children. At that moment she did not want more children. They had named their son Patrick. Janelle felt jinxed when they buried that little boy. It had been four years until Janelle conceived again.

226

Her elation was uncontrollable when the doctor told her she was finally pregnant. It had been an easy pregnancy and the twins were born perfect. No health issues and no worries. They were strong, healthy babies. They didn't bring back their brother they would never know, but they certainly brought meaning to Logan and Janelle's life.

"Hi honey, where is David?" Janelle asked wondering where Lacey's twin was.

"He is with Dad. They are finishing trying to tie David's tie. He can't get it right and Dad is trying to help him. It is like a comedy act, Mom. You should really go rescue them both." She was beaming and looked lovely in her burgundy dress. "Mom you look like an angel. Dad is going to freak when he sees how pretty you are tonight." Lacey sat on the bed and smiled at her mother. "Oh, guess what? Jake is here!" She had almost forgotten because he had gone out to the barn to look in on the horses. "I didn't know he was coming. I thought he said he couldn't get away."

Kelly had passed away when Jake was twelve and he had come to live with Logan and Janelle. He was a brilliant boy. He had finished high school midway through his junior year. He was now twenty-four years old and had just finished law school. Janelle was so proud of him.

"It is going to be a perfect evening, Lacey. With all of us together. Well, except Grandma and Grandpa. I miss them so much tonight." Janelle tried to stop the tears welling in her eyes.

"Oh Momma." Lacey hugged her mother and knew she couldn't let her ruin her make up. "Let's go rescue Dad and David before they hang themselves."

***

The tables in the lower restaurant at Shannon's Luck

were all decorated with white linen table cloths, white roses and candles. It was beautiful. Logan knew that it would make Janelle smile. That had been his favorite thing to do for twenty years. Twenty years, he was thinking to himself that had flown by. He knew Janelle would be coming with Jake. He had wanted her to show up last so there would be nothing for her to do. Jake accommodated by coming up with an excuse to take longer to get ready than Logan and the twins did.

Sarah, Mitch and Zoe arrived and hugged Logan and the twins. Sarah had not remained the beauty she had been twenty plus years ago, but Mitch looked at her as if the sun rose and set in her eyes. Logan understood the feeling. Life had been good to them.

"She's here!" Frank announced as he slowly, slowly made his way down the stairs. Logan went to help him get to his seat. Lacey, David and Zoe lit all the candles and everyone sat at their tables. The center table, next to the fireplace, had a full bouquet of white roses and white and yellow daisies. This was where Janelle would sit with her husband of twenty years. They were well into their forty's now and Logan was thrilled that he was going to gift her with a fourteen day cruise on the great sail ship around the Greek Isles. She had always wanted to go, but they had never had the time, or the children had been too young, or a hundred other excuses Janelle always had when Logan told her they should plan the cruise. Not tonight. Tonight she would have no excuses. In two weeks they would be on their way. Sarah was going to stay in town with the twins and everything was going to be perfect for Logan and Janelle as they took their anniversary cruise.

***

Jake held Janelle's arm as they walked into the bar at Shannon's Luck. "Everyone must be downstairs Jake." Janelle was so proud of him. He was a handsome and brilliant young man. His mother would have loved who he had become. Janelle felt a twinge of pain for all Kelly had lost in not getting to see her gangly pre-teenaged boy grow into such an accomplished and handsome young man.

"Come on Mom," Jake said. He had called her 'Mom' from the day he told Logan and Janelle he wanted to be adopted. He had told Logan he hated calling him Uncle. He told Logan he was the only Dad he ever had. He fell into Janelle's arms and asked her if she wanted to be his mother. The three sat on the floor and cried together for Jake's loss of his own mother. The adoption process began the following week.

Jake escorted Janelle down the stairs. As she walked down the last step she saw a bright glow. As she turned and saw everyone she loved sitting at the elegant tables with the flowers and candles, she was speechless. She brought her hands together at her mouth and made an overwhelming happy sound.

Logan stood and said "Happy Anniversary,

Janelle." Everyone clapped and sung their well wishes to the couple.

Logan walked over and took Janelle's arm to escort her to the table. Dinner was catered for the family and it was an incredible feast.

After dinner and desert, while everyone was enjoying their drinks and coffee, Logan tapped his wine glass and said he had an announcement. He stood and took Janelle's hand to draw her up to stand beside him.

"Janelle, I have loved you from the moment I saw you. I loved you before I ever saw you, but the moment I saw you, my love made sense. We have had a good life together that has grown from the good times and the really ugly and painful times. We have incredible family." He smiled at the family sitting around them. "We have three incredible kids. You have been a devoted mother and a devoted wife. Shannon's Luck is a blessed place for having shared your attentions for so many years. This Shannon..."

Logan said touching his chest and speaking of himself, "has never had so much luck as the day you agreed to be my wife. I want to give you something you have always deserved, but would never accept." He handed her the small gold wrapped package.

"Oh Logan. Thank you." She wrapped her arms around him. He still took her breath away when she touched him and he held her and the scent of him permeated her being. She could not wait to tell him her surprise.

"You don't even know what it is, Baby. Open it!" He smiled at her. She was always gracious. He loved that about her. "Open it."

Janelle sat and unwrapped the small box. She saw the front of the tickets which bore a photo of the gorgeous Sailing Flagship that she recognized as a ship from the Greek Isles Cruise Line. "Oh Logan! Logan, is it...?" She jumped into his arms.

"Yes, honey. We are going on your cruise. You do deserve it and you are going!" He hugged her while she thanked him repeatedly. Everyone clapped.

"Logan. I have two gifts for you. Both are in this envelope." She handed him a Manilla envelope that had his name written in calligraphy on the front. The first paper was an ownership deed to an Arabian horse that Logan had wanted to buy, but wouldn't spend the money on since it was only for him to enjoy and not for working the ranch.

"Oh Janelle. Wow, baby." He couldn't believe she had purchased the horse. He knew someone had bought her because he had called again just last week to see if the horse was still available. It wasn't, but the owner said nothing more. "You are quite sneaky my love. Thank you." He kissed her.

"Keep looking in the envelope Logan. There is another surprise in there." Janelle was nervous. She knew how much Logan loved her and had wanted more children, but wasn't sure how he was going to react at this stage in their lives. She wanted him to be as happy as she was.

He raised his eyebrows twice in boyish delight. He pulled the grainy photo out of the envelope and looked at it confused. He looked at her and when he saw the hope and happiness in her eyes, he looked at the photo again. It hit him. Logan let out a "whoop" sound and grabbed Janelle and spun her around. He kissed her and told her repeatedly how much he loved her.

"Hey you two," Sarah exclaimed. "Let the rest of us in on this great surprise."

"Sarah, everyone. We are having a baby." Logan was beaming like the proud father he already was, and the proud father he would be again.

Everyone laughed and clapped, and jumped to hug the couple. This was a perfect ending to their twentieth anniversary. It was an even more perfect beginning to the next chapter of their lives.

***

Seven months later a perfect baby girl was born. She was healthy and had a head full of blond curls. Janelle and Logan knew they would probably fall out, but she was stunning as she smiled at her parents. People would have thought the couple too old to become parents again. Janelle and Logan knew that love didn't have to fit into anyone's given ideas of what was acceptable. This baby showed them and anyone else, that love always returned to itself and always refused to be ignored.

They named their daughter 'Emma.'

As they started home Logan told Janelle that he had heard from Jake earlier that morning.

"Apparently he has a big surprise to tell us. He will be here this evening. I wonder what he has to tell us."

Logan and Janelle had become parents again that week. Little did they know their family and their love was soon to be increased again. Jake Logan and his bride of four months, Amanda, were going to have a baby of their own. Jake could not wait to tell his mom and dad. He knew that they would be elated for him. Jake had been through a lot of disappointment and pain in his life, but that was all about to end with the birth of his child in the near future. He knew that his parents had taught him how to love well and how to stick to a commitment. He and Amanda were the next great love story, he just knew it. Soon, Janelle and Logan would know it too.

***

Several months later the newest "Logan" family member arrived. Jake and Amanda named their son Shannon Patrick Logan. Jake explained it was after his birth father, his grandpa and his dad, Shannon. Their baby was a welcome addition to the 'Logan' family.

Shannon's Luck continued to live on and live forward. The happiness and love of the challenges and commitment to marriages, raising children and growing old together continued itself for the Logan family as passionately as if none of it had ever happened before.

THE END

Made in the USA
Charleston, SC
20 December 2016